Watch for the

Whirlwinds

Noel Barton

Cover design by Linda Garcia
Cover editing by Robin Kinser, Josh Arnold, Jessica Hampton
Cover photography by Carol Barton

Table of Contents

Foreword

Historical fiction is fiction mixed with fact. Its design is to help the reader become a part of the narrative by recalling similar events in one's life, to become part of the story, and to learn from the action. Carol Barton has managed to tell a wonderful story of times past. She has very ably woven a remarkable story that involves the reader in the events. You will find yourself living in the action in a "hard to put down" story. In addition, her ability to weave moral lessons and scriptural truths throughout the story, allows one to be entertained and educated. "Watch for the Whirlwinds" is one of the best stories I have ever read. It is a story that one would enjoy reading (and learning from) a second time. I heartily recommend this to all ages.

Joe Causey
Retired Pastor
Providence Knob Baptist Church

Chapter One

Meryl's First Never

"**S**OLD FOR A dollar bill!" the auctioneer's shout echoed louder than his pounding gavel or the noise in the room.

"You're one lucky man, Buck; got that rabbit trap for a dollar!" a rival bidder bragged, giving the winner a slap on the back.

"Meryl, come here to me!" my father's voice thundered, causing a hush to spread over the crowd.

Ol' Buck might have been lucky, but my luck was about to run out, as it had many times before. "D-a-a-a-d-d-y, what did I do?" I whined, knowing my pleading was in vain.

"Come here to me," he repeated, sliding a thick leather belt through his pant loops. His large, calloused hand gripped my small arm to position me for my beating.

A stream of urine puddled on the floor as I danced from the pain of the first strike. A second, third, and fourth strike followed. Afterward, I stumbled to my mother's arms, under the eyes of the shocked, yet curious, dispersing audience. Lashes on my legs, back and buttocks throbbed with pain. My tear-streaked cheeks burned from humiliation, and again I smelled of urine.

I seldom understood what sent Daddy into a rage. This time I had accidentally passed between old Buck and the auctioneer. I was one of several children who had taken that same path; however, I was the only one punished. A bid had been successfully placed, yet my dad could not pass up an opportunity to demonstrate the power he held over his family. The need to flaunt his macho image, fueled by the beers in his belly, nearly always ruled.

He loved the Monday night auctions, mostly for the power play. As proof, he had a collection of useless items purchased solely for satisfying his need to win.

Larson Strom's reputation for an unpredictable, violent temper was well known. People were reluctant to out-bid him for fear it would surface, even at a community auction sale. Ol' Buck's streak of luck was only there because Daddy hunted coons and not rabbits.

My mother could do nothing but stand aside and cringe as each blow cut into my flesh. She saw bringing first aid or a change of clothing for me as an invitation to his outbursts. She lived in a state of part denial, part false hope that each rampage would be his last.

When not drinking, Daddy could be a loving father but his being an alcoholic, made those times fewer than any of us would have liked. His fiery temper was always just beneath the surface and could all too quickly rise to the top.

Again, I'd wear my urine soaked clothes until he decided the night was done. The swollen bruises could last for a week or more; the emotional scars would last a lifetime.

The final item was sold. Once we were allowed to leave, we found ourselves at the mercy of a drunken driver. Mama knew better than to request to drive us home. In his condition, his wrath could have been turned toward her or more frightening, toward an innocent bystander. She silently prayed for God's protection—one more time.

The car lunged into our driveway, nearly throwing me into the floorboard. Daddy staggered drunkenly into the house, leaving Mama with the struggle of getting me out and into the house. Lugging my five year old pudgy body had become increasingly difficult for her. Avoiding the welts and bruises that reached from the middle of my back to the calves of my legs was an even bigger challenge.

For nearly six years, my mother had been witness to those egotistical, selfish displays of violence. She had not been overly concerned that he was drinking the first night they met. She figured a little drink now and then wasn't so bad. She had been incredibly naïve. A handsome, muscular man, fresh out of the army in 1945, he'd always known how to work a crowd. She fell for him during one of his signature performances of bending a tire-tool in half. She was also gratified to find that he was equally taken with her.

Beautiful had never been most people's description of my mother, Mary Edna Madden. Homely would not have fit either. On occasion she allowed a warm smile that projected an inner beauty not easily ignored, or sometimes, understood. Definite facial lines and prematurely graying hair resulted from years of impulsive poor choices and their consequences. A few extra pounds supported by a large frame made her a woman that would not attract most men.

My mother was a self-made woman who stemmed from humble beginnings in Kosciusko, Mississippi. She had a past she had never tried to hide, yet wasn't anxious to reveal. She suffered the disgrace of being a fourteen year old mother of an illegitimate child in 1922. Her loyal family faithfully helped her, though the shadows of shame also fell across each of them.

Escaping the endless whispers and dissecting eyes had been hopeless; the somewhat self-righteous, but God-fearing community, considered her 'fallen from Grace,' and she was marked as a 'bad girl' with a bastard son. Her child forever tried to rise above the label of illegitimacy while she wrestled with a shame that society refused to forgive. Her mother and father tackled the task of raising him, while continuing to rear his young mother, although they never tried to mask the circumstances of his birth. Their honest approach was admirable to many but abhorrent to others; this only adding to their shame.

Despite her physical imperfections, there was an air about this so-called 'bad girl' that captured the interest of even a casual observer. Maybe it was how she would tilt her head and squarely looked into another's eyes. Maybe it was that worldly, 'don't-mess-with-me attitude' she projected. My dad was drawn to whatever it was, and she enjoyed pulling the rope. He was not one to judge others, possibly because fingers could quickly be pointed back toward him.

She flourished on his attention and affection. He thrived on her boundless, forgiving love that was willing to look beyond his flaws and lifted him to an even higher dimension, at least to one that was seen through her eyes.

The attraction and dysfunction of this union between my parents set the stage for my roller coaster type life with its ups and downs, tears and laughter, loves and losses, and the people who ultimately shared my ride. It's been as though the whirlwinds that accompanied the April showers on the day of my birth are following me—still.

Chapter Two

The Move and...Meryl's Shadow

FOR THE NEXT eight years, the rollercoaster pattern of my life continued. As most families, we had our share of happy moments along with the bad. At times, my dad could light up a room. Other times, he could shut it down. Occasionally, when things were good, he'd suggest we go out for an ice cream cone after our evening meal, or drop by to visit his brother and their large family. Both suggestions were treats for me. Naturally, I loved ice cream, but being an only child, I also loved the family visits with my seven cousins. I felt elated and almost normal, that our happy family was visiting their happy family.

Nevertheless, Mama and I were silently aware that at any time, an unforeseen incident could thrust him into a state of rage. A pleasant game of cards with his brother and sister-in-law could erupt into an unwarranted display of discipline, resulting in a belt lashing for me and a pushing and yelling match with my mother.

One memorable evening, my parents were invited to have a friendly card game of Canasta with Uncle Bray and Aunt Gwen who had the seven children. The adults were playing cards at the kitchen table. I was in the living room with my rowdy cousins. Bray Jr., their oldest son, while standing upon their living room sofa, declared himself to be, 'king of the mountain' while his siblings tried to overpower him. The jumping, scuffling and laughing became extremely disturbing to the foursome engrossed in their now third game of Canasta. I wasn't jumping on the furniture or scuffling, but was sitting on the arm of an over-stuffed chair and laughing along with the others. Without warning, my dad stormed into the room, grabbed my arm, swung me around, and began flailing me with his folded belt. As usual, the urine slowly began to trickle down my legs. Not only was I in pain, but I was overwhelmingly embarrassed as well. At once, the others, along with the dethroned king, each found a resting place, and the room became silent, except for my sniffling.

Daddy returned to the game table, feeling he had taken care of the problem by making an example of me. Mama came to console me and wipe up the puddle I had created. She whispered for me to try to be quiet, that we should be leaving soon. It wasn't long until the cousins started a different game that again became noisy. I wasn't going to take any more chances. I found a book and a corner in the hall completely away from the group. I was probably safe by that time though; Daddy had already clearly made his statement, by his outburst.

After a few drinks too many, he could react the

same if I accidentally dropped or spilled a beverage. On another evening, we were at Uncle Paul's and Aunt Jacquelyn's home for a visit. My mom and Aunt Jackie were rustling up a few refreshments for us. I wanted to help by stirring some Kool-aid in my aunt's new glass pitcher. Eagerly, I began stirring too briskly, and the pitcher broke. Glass shattered everywhere, spilling their last package of Kool-aid, making a sticky mess. Although it was an accident and I was only trying to be helpful, this incident also resulted in another embarrassing belt-whipping for me.

Our family tension ultimately took its toll on my emotional well-being. I began to have nightmares, nervously bite my nails, over-eat, and occasionally, I wet my bed.

Overcompensating for Daddy's actions any way she could, my mother would constantly try to offer words of comfort and encouragement. She never hesitated to push me into the spotlight, and to take advantage of every possible opportunity to reinforce my self-esteem. Both she and Daddy took pride in my singing talent. I could usually gain an audience after only three or four words into a song.

The love my mother had for me was undeniable. I also always knew that Daddy loved me and my mother, in his own way. Regrettably, while he was under the influence of alcohol, his actions could overshadow the evidence of any love he had for either of us, almost beyond recognition.

Edna, it was strange that even the most ordinary,

unflattering name, sounded beautiful if it was attached to someone you loved. I sometimes questioned why, with a pretty name such as Mary, my mother was called Edna. I realize now that Edna was a bolder, more fitting name for her since she projected boldness. She wasn't overbearing but mindfully soft spoken and easy to be around. People respected that about her. That was— everyone but my dad. He acquired a respect for her years after her death—but by then it was too late.

She was nine years older than he. To some, that alone could have been viewed as a potential marital problem. However, it was not. Her less-than hour glass figure might have thrown some men a curve but it never lessened Daddy's attraction for her. He loved her as much as he was ever capable of loving any woman. He confessed his love for her to me, in years to come. I just wish he had confessed it to her, when she needed most to hear it.

The pattern continued until the spring of 1959: then my life roller-coaster jumped the track. My mother was diagnosed with uterine cancer. Daddy leaned on his bottle even more heavily, while trying to mask the fear he felt at the threat of losing his wife and the mother of his child. He looked for every possible excuse to be away from her and his home, in an effort to escape the reality of facing her imminent death. There seemed to constantly be someone who needed him to work on their vehicle. There were more coon hunting escapades with his buddies than usual. He even volunteered for over-time at work, which was not a common practice in the past. Unfortunately, for him, and for my mother, those hours and days of avoidance could never be revisited.

Looking back now, even at thirteen years old, I see I should have realized that my mother was dying of cancer. However, during the entire span of her illness, I was never told anything but that she would be well again. I witnessed the strength and refuge of my youth slowly crumbling, as she grew weaker and finally became bedridden. Nonetheless, the doctors, my family, and even my mother gave me the false hope that she would survive.

I would often lie next to her after arriving home from school. We talked about me, my day, and all else, but her sickness and possible death never crossed either of our lips. I know now that she was always in denial, as was I.

During her funeral, there were no words, songs or embraces that could give me enough comfort to make the emptiness disappear. That couldn't have been my mother in that casket. My mother was warm, loving, and all consumed with me. Whatever it was in that steel box was cold, expressionless, and totally oblivious to my horror at the moment.

"I know how you feel, dear," whispered my mother's friend Nola as she slipped into the pew and cradled me in her arms.

No! She couldn't have possibly known how I felt. She was a grown woman. I was a child. That wasn't her mother that they are getting ready to put into the ground. How could Nola have known what I was feeling?

After much endless babbling, Nola eventually, stumbled upon the words I needed to hear. She was finally right; I had to be brave. My mother had carried a shield of courage up until the end of her life, when death forced her to lay it down. Now, I would have to pick it up and carry on as she did.

At the graveside service I was handed a rose from one of her bouquets. Mourners filed by one after another with handshakes, hugs, teary eyes, and faces of concern. Friends and family questioned why God would have taken my devoted mother at a time when it would seem that I needed her the most and left me with my dad, who most of them saw only as a drunkard. Finally, the last car sped away, carrying its occupants back to their briefly interrupted lives, leaving Daddy and me to sort out what remained of ours.

Four months after Mama's death and having to shift me back and forth from one relative to another, Daddy became very frustrated. He worked the evening shift at a local paint factory. I was too young to stay alone at night. A few times on the weekends, when relatives saw my visits as an inconvenience and, rightly so, as they all had their own families to contend with, he dragged me along with him to the taverns. I think if haunting someone is possible after death, my mother surely haunted Daddy for that! Eventually, he decided it was time we should move elsewhere. I would be taken to Missouri to live with my grandmother, allowing him to do what came as second nature, run away from his problems.

One Friday afternoon, after receiving his weekly paycheck, he burst into the house, announced that he'd quit his job, and then started barking orders for the packing to begin. On his way home, he made one of his regular stops at the liquor store for a pint of whiskey. By the time he arrived, he was feeling its effects quite nicely and was ready to head to Grandma's house as soon as our car could be packed.

As far back as I could remember, hardly any of our trips to Grandma's house had been preplanned. He usually came home and gave my mother the packing command. She scurried around, grabbing what she could, stuffed it into a bag, and off we'd go. If she took longer than he liked, he could purposely make our journey an extremely unpleasant one. The difference, this time I was doing the scurrying, and this time it was a move, not a visit.

While struggling with the reality of being a motherless child, I was being forced to face yet another. The home still warmed by her touch would be cold and deserted. Only an arm chair, a bed, a place at the kitchen table would be home for the ghost of one loved so dearly. Who would place a flower on her grave?

On earlier trips, it had never been my job to do the packing. I worried if I had gathered the important things or left them behind in our deserted shell of a home. While darting from room to room, I had tried to decide what items Mama would have considered most important.

Mama's trunk, about three feet wide and a little over two feet in height, was the first item I secured. It needed to be given a place of priority in the car, because of its size; other things could later be squeezed in around it. The old trunk had once belonged to Mama's mother, who died almost twenty-five years before I was born. Throughout her life, Mama carefully preserved both the trunk and its contents. I now had to do the same.

I had watched many times as my mother packed and repacked that cedar lined trunk, as she shared detailed facts and stories with me about it contents. The exterior was made of hickory, covered with embossed leather, scrolled with tiny, delicate rose vines. The entire structure was hugged by two thin metal bands on each side of a brass latch engraved with the initial M as if to further protect the special treasures inside. It suddenly occurred to me that the M could stand for Meryl, as well as Madden, since the trunk was now mine.

A dome lid provided space for a wooden tray designed with various compartments for particulars such as coins, jewelry and a few war medallions. There was ample space underneath the tray for all of Mama's other special treasures.

It was as though my mother somehow knew she wouldn't be there for my future. She taught me the names of those pictured in an old family album and explained their connection to me. While holding a pair of black high-heeled slippers, she shared the story of the evening her mother died and how she slipped them off, rolled down her gartered, knee-length stockings into little balls, and tucked them neatly inside the slippers. She then retied the shoelaces and placed them beneath the edge of her deathbed, saying she would never need to wear them again. To this day, the laces have never been untied, nor have the stockings ever been removed. I noted how small my grandmother's feet were. I definitely didn't take after her in that characteristic.

I had often watched as my mother ran her fingertips over a little dress and under slip that she hand-sewed for me before I was born and I remembered the light of her smile as if reflecting the glowing love within each stitch.

Every time the lid of that old trunk was opened, each fragrance trapped within would escape as if rushing to tell its own unique story. My Great-grandfather's worn leather-bound Bible, that contained names, dates of births, marriages and deaths, along with special, bookmarked passages, a pair of quilting cards that had a little cotton still pressed between them, a stack of old newspapers tied with ribbons, and my first baby shoes, size 00, that Mama had bronzed for preservation, were few among the many items in the trunk. I closed my eyes and opened the lid, one more time before packing it away, to savor the musky aromas and tried to recall all the stories that linked me to the sweet memories of my mother. A part of her has always been intertwined around each item inside that old trunk. Before finally closing the lid, I added the newest treasure; the flower given to me at her funeral that I had folded and pressed in wax paper and slid inside the pages of her family

Bible.

I left to find a blanket to wrap and protect the trunk from anything we would need to stack on top or around it. Without Daddy knowing, when I reentered the room, I saw him as he brushed his hand awkwardly but tenderly over the trunk's lid. At that time, I realized that although he never admitted it, Daddy too, had special connections and affection for the trunk and its legacy. He knew how special it had been to Mama and also what it would mean to me in years to come.

"You ready to pack this old thing in the car?" He asked, trying to sound as though he was unattached to the idea. After that, I no longer worried that he would balk about it taking up so much space, when I told him it was ready to go.

I cautiously packed a collection of carnival glass bowls, etched juice glasses and a gold, rimmed cup and saucer set that I was told would be mine some day. Well—this was someday and they were mine now. I didn't think of it at the time, but I wished I had gathered an article or two of Mama's clothing, just for the keeping. Then I remembered: I barely had time to get any of my own!

As soon as we crammed everything that would possibly fit into our small sedan, we hit the road. An unlocked house with furniture and contents still in place was left behind. We sped away like thieves, with no pang of conscience for our actions. Little did I know that *thief* was a pretty accurate description of us. Daddy left all debts behind unpaid, with no indication as to where he could be reached. Being reached was the last thing he wanted. He had no intention at that time, of getting a real job or of building any solid structure in his life. I was the only thing that stood between him and the open road. He was taking me to his elderly mother for her to reckon with, to allow him the freedom to be free.

Tears slid down my cheeks paralleling the rain drops that had found their way down the car window. Haphazard drops, whirled by the wind, pooled along the window's edge. I thought of how I resembled those raindrops; I too, was being helplessly blown by an uncontrollable wind of fate. Staring into the darkness, I kept my back to Daddy, hoping to avoid an explanation of my tears. I wasn't sure I could have explained. Perhaps they could have been the spillage of sadness from my mother's bitter cup. Maybe they were an emotional backlash of being ripped from anything comforting or familiar. They might have been the product of the absolute fear of my unknown future.

Those who knew him would have thought that if Daddy had an attachment to anything other than me, it would have been his coon dogs. If that was true, the attachment was a shallow one. Not long after he arrived home, a truck appeared in our driveway to collect Daddy's dogs. He sold them to a coon hunting buddy and threw the puppies in to sweeten the deal.

I was being returned to my birthplace in the Boo-theel of Missouri. I hardly remembered ever living there. My dad, being a rolling stone, never stayed anywhere for very long. I was not sure when we moved, but I remembered my first school experience to be in Michigan. By fourth grade, I had attended two schools in Michigan, one in Florida, along with two other schools in Illinois.

Daddy's stint at his last job allowed me to attend the same school consecutively for three years. That school hadn't provided an overwhelming sense of happiness, but at least I knew what and what not to expect.

A new school was likely to present a new set of challenges. Elementary school children in the 50s and 60s were rarely overweight. For me, it was not what I *was*—*but* what I *wasn't*. I wasn't one of those wispy, thin children whose chronological age matched their dress size. I wasn't overly large, but I was heavier than most. Children as a rule are cruel and painfully honest concerning things that are different about their peers. God help the child who was grossly overweight! As for me, how many ways could I be tortured because I cast a *larger shadow* than most children my age? Sometimes, that *shadow* was my only friend.

OUR DESTINATION WAS Muddy Ox, Missouri, a former logging camp, now cotton community, located in the southern part of the Missouri Bootheel. The town gained its name when it was initially settled. Oxen, with their split hoofs, could tread the gumbo mud and pull the supply wagons used in the town's construction without getting stuck. Too many teams of mules were lost due to exhaustion after getting bogged down in almost knee-deep mud, because their solid hoofs would act as suction cups in such conditions. Also, the yokes of the oxen wouldn't get tangled in the dense brush as did the mules' harnesses. The massive beasts were entirely mud covered at the end of a day's work of clearing the untamed, watery woodlands; therefore the town was named, Muddy Ox.

In the beginning, the only way in or out of Muddy Ox was by rail cars and a primitive pole road which was made of log poles cut to equal lengths, laid side by side, forming a road that stretched eastward to the neighboring village of Doodlum Switch. A gated fence, which was securely locked from dusk to dawn, protected the entire town from wild animals such as wolves, wild hogs, panthers, wild dogs, and an unconfirmed rumor of black bears. It was common practice at that time for most men to carry some type of gun for protection.

Only a portion of the gated fence still remains near the church as a reminder of the struggles endured by their brave ancestors who were determined to establish the town of Muddy Ox. Then and now, with the exception of one blacktop road running through the middle of town, all other roads in and around the community are gravel or dirt.

Muddy Ox is a small village, consisting of eight blocks on the west side of the main gravel road that connects it to 84 Highway. The school, big store, post office, cotton gin, gas station, and other businesses, allow it to be loosely called a town. One Methodist Church, attended by the majority of folks, graces the edge of Muddy Ox proper, until this day.

My grandmother's house sat on the east side of the main gravel road, in the portion of Muddy Ox referred to as Silver Leaf. This area was rightly named because there was at least one silver-leaf maple tree in almost every yard. Silver Leaf consisted of a corner store followed by three blocks of modest houses with neatly groomed yards. One of those was soon to be my new home.

Grandma's house was on the back corner lot of the third block. On the front side, facing the main gravel road lived the three McCrady girls: Scarlett Estelle, Melanie Ann, and Tara Gayle. Their mother had an obsession with the novel, *Gone with the Wind*, and named her daughters after the main characters and places in the book. They were Grandma's neighbors and were always welcome playmates during our frequent visits throughout my childhood. Now, they would be not only my friends and new neighbors, but also my schoolmates. Unlike my so-called friends in Illinois, Scar, Melly Ann, or Tara Gayle never called me fat or other belittling names.

I was plagued with various questions concerning this move. Would my other future classmates be as kind as the McCrady sisters had always been? Visiting Grandma was one thing, but how would it be to live with her? As far as I knew, Grandma had no idea we were coming to visit, let alone move in. Extending the courtesy of advance notice in anything he did was out of character for my dad. How would Grandma feel about our move? Would her welcome be as warm when she discovered Daddy was coming jobless?

The last two questions should not have been concerns for a thirteen year old. Those details should have been worked out before Daddy forced our move.

This was my transition from child to adult. From then on, the adult thinking was mine; Daddy wasn't capable of it. I learned later, he never had been. The one buried six feet under the ground with the grave markings 'Mother' was the adult. It was Mama who had kept our family unit together, in spite of him. He never saw the importance of stability. We had a roof over our head, food to eat, and his prize coon dogs were in a pen out back. He had a car to get us where we needed to go. There was always enough money for gas and a pint of whiskey to hide under the front seat of his car.

By his standards, Daddy was doing all right. Now all he needed was the whiskey and the money to buy another one when that one was gone. This was the right thing to do as far as he saw. Mama had loved and admired his mom. Why, living with Grandma in a good Christian home would have surely been what she would have wanted for me.

Grandma was a God-fearing woman who could—and would—quote Scripture to fit any situation. She never missed an opportunity to let Daddy know she wanted him to follow her example. I would be kept in school and, no doubt, taught the right way to live. He was confident she would share enough of her monthly pension check to provide me with all of the necessities: food, bed, four walls. Why, from his point of view, he was actually doing her a favor! She'd lived alone, since his father; my Grandpa Omar, had died the year before; now she'd have me to keep her company. She had always been especially fond of me. This move would just be the best for everyone. He was sure of it.

THE REAL TRUTH was neatly hidden behind those comforting thoughts. In reality, it was best for him. He wanted no responsibility, and this would be the way to not have any. I would realize in years to come that I had been literally dumped on my Grandmother's porch, much like a stray cat, with only my clothes and potential in hand.

It was after midnight when we pulled into her yard. One of my worries was proven unnecessary. It didn't matter how late it was or that we woke her. Grandma still met us with open arms and a warm smile.

I found a comfortable place on the end of her couch as Daddy presented his plan to an unsuspecting mother. She had many questions, and I wanted to hear the answers, but as hard as I tried, I couldn't stay awake.

I barely recalled giving into sleep the next morning when I found myself still on the couch, a pillow under my head and a light blanket draped over me. The last thing I remembered was the rhythmic ticking of an eight-day wall clock while Grandma questioned what my mother might have wished.

Daddy didn't waste any time. After breakfast, he backed as close to the front porch as his back bumper would allow and unloaded our life's possessions. The three of us stood in awe at the amount of *stuff* that could be packed into one small car. Grandma worried *where on earth* she would find room for all of it in her small, one-bedroom house. I was already remembering things I'd left behind. It was too late by then. Illinois might as well have been a million miles away.

Anything left behind wasn't Daddy's problem. He wanted his car unloaded and ready for him to leave in whatever direction it was pointed. He did just that, once the last item was out and heaped in a pile on the porch. He hugged us both, promised he'd be in touch to send money, as soon as he could. Then, he was off.

Grandma went into the house, mumbling something about a bite to eat. I sat on the edge of the porch, staring at the ruts left by the car carrying my only parent away to who knew where. I wondered—as Grandma had the night before—what my mother would think about our sudden move.

My mind wandered back to happier times when I was very small. I couldn't have been more than three or four. I was young enough that my mother allowed me to run around the yard, bare foot, wearing nothing but a pair of white, cotton panties because it was so hot and sultry.

I was fascinated with Grandma's chickens and loved to chase them around the yard. I didn't want to hurt them. I just liked to see them squawk and run. Grandma didn't want me to chase her chickens, especially her laying hens. She feared that I would scare them so badly that they wouldn't lay any eggs.

"Alice, Meryl is chasing your chickens again," my Grandpa Omar tattled.

"I think I know how to break her from doing that," Grandma said, as she approached me.

She gathered the old red rooster up in her apron and lightly raked his spurs against my bare shoulder, hoping it would scare me. She said he would scratch me with his spurs and be mad at me for bothering his hens.

"Meryl, I will scratch you if you keep chasing my hens, URRRR," she gave the rooster a growling, animated voice while barely touching my skin with his claw.

I could remember this vividly. I was such a little actress. I cried and pretended that I believed her. Putting the rooster down and feeling as though she had broken me of the habit of chasing her chickens forever, she took me by the hand and led me to my mother for her to reinforce the warning.

"Did that old rooster get mad and scratch you, Baby?" my mother asked as she lifted me to her lap.

"Noooo… Grandma made that rooster do that," I pouted.

"There's no foolin' that youngun'. She's too smart," said Grandpa Omar.

Everyone laughed, including me. Mama set me down and I went back to playing in the yard. I didn't chase Grandma's chickens again, but not because of her or the rooster.

"Don't be chasing your Grandma's chickens anymore, Baby," Daddy said with authority as he slapped me on the back of my leg with a force powerful enough to cause me to stumble. He didn't use his belt this time, but the sting of his hand made enough of an impression that I didn't want any more of that.

My uncanny sense of reasoning was superior to that of most children my age. It allowed me to see the end result of situations. In this case, I reasoned that the stinging slap from my dad could become a greater demonstration of discipline if I didn't learn a little self-control. Where was that reasoning power now? It had deserted me. I surely couldn't reason or act my way out of this last turn of events. Mama was dead. Daddy was gone, and it was just Grandma and me now.

My thoughts were interrupted by the frantic squawking of an old hen in the chicken pen, calling her baby chick to safety. The wayward chick ran to snuggle beneath her wing, and all was quiet again. I wished I could be like that little chick, feel my mother's comforting embrace and hear her voice again. In reality, sad as it may be, neither I nor anyone else would ever again, hear my mother's voice.

The ruts left across Grandma's front yard were symbolic of the ruts dug into Daddy's disorderly life. His marriage to my mother and having a child weren't the sources of Daddy's problems. His drinking and flawed desires to have anything were his problems. He had a definite split personality. He'd give a person the shirt off his back, but heaven help anyone who tried to take it. He'd share food or money with anyone, even to his own family's detriment, as long as the sharing was his idea. If a mechanic was needed, he was near genius. If it took muscle to get something done, he had that! This was his positive side.

His negative side screamed selfishness. He'd scratch anyone's back as long as that action didn't interfere with his own itch. He never put what should be priorities in any logical order such as jobs, home, schools, relationships, and, obviously, parental obligations. All of these could be found at the bottom of his list, far beneath his own desires.

As Daddy drove away from Grandma and me that morning, no doubt he was experiencing emotions he'd never felt before. He was lonely, confused, and, as hard as it was for him to admit, scared. He was doing what he'd always done, avoiding obligations and yielding to the demons of alcohol, temper, and selfishness.

Truthfully, I had seen his negative side often enough that I was semi-willing and somewhat relieved to let him go. In many ways he would behave like a disobedient child. I saw my mother try to combat his will often enough that I feared I didn't have what it took to meet that challenge.

I also wouldn't miss his hard side. That was the side that bought me boy's oxfords because my feet were too wide and then forced me to wear them to school. In his opinion, girl shoes became stretched and worn much too quickly. Surely, he would have made an effort to find me more acceptable shoes, if only once he had been witness to the embarrassment and abuse I took at school because he forced me to wear 'boy' shoes. Surely, he would have bought his only child new shoes as often as needed, if he had seen and heard the ridicule. Effort spent and the cost of buying more fashionable shoes for me would have been totally insignificant compared to what it cost me in self-esteem.

It was my hope to *never* have to wear boy shoes again! I had a lot of *nevers* in my life. *Never* again would I have to endure the cruel jeering of those horrible children at that school. *Never* again would I be subjected to the numbness of uncaring teachers who turned deaf ears from stabbing verbal attacks. Most of all, I hoped and prayed *never* again to wear the cuts and bruises from a drunkard's belt. No, I would not miss his hard side at all.

Difficult as it was to believe, I would miss the dad I wanted him to be. The one that he was just often enough to make me love him. Children want to love their parents even if they're scared to death of them. I would miss the surety that, with him around, nothing but he could harm me. He *did* give me a little money from time to time. He *could* fix most things when they were broken. And, on a good day, he hugged and made me feel loved the way a dad should make his daughter feel.

Chapter Three

Sorting the Pile on the Porch

"**Y**OU READY FOR some dinner?" I was not sure how long Grandma had been standing in the door behind me, but she was anxious to do one of the things she liked best: fix a situation with food. Grandma referred to the three daily meals as breakfast, dinner and supper. A Southerner's noon meal was called dinner. Lunch was a term reserved only for 'Yankees.'

My grandma, Alice Strom, wasn't a large woman, but she had a strong build. She had shrunk a bit over the years and her legs were slightly bowed. For a sixty-seven year old, there was very little gray in the coal black hair that she wore pulled back into a neat little bun. Natural smile lines accented her small, puckered mouth. Her snappy brown eyes were most noticeable, as though if you looked hard enough, you could see down into her heart and soul.

Pictures of her when she was younger, proved her to be quite beautiful. A soft beauty still remained about her, especially when she smiled. She was known for being highly intelligent and quick witted. Engaging in conversation with her didn't offer a clue that you were speaking with a person who had never attended school a day in her life.

Out of sheer necessity, she had learned to read and write enough to get by. One could read anything she wrote by sounding out the words because she spelled everything just as it sounded to her. On occasion, she resorted to folk terms, but for the most part, she spoke nearly proper English.

She sometimes had the habit of assigning a word to a situation that didn't apply, except only to her. One word was *bitable*. She used that word to describe a person who was easy to get along with. She said they wouldn't bite you with their words or actions. I learned sometime later that the actual word is biddable, meaning one who is docile or pliable. She had the definition close to correct, but pronounced and spelled it to fit her use of the word. Most people, however, used other words to describe those who were congenial. To her, people who overreacted to situations were said to have hysterics, as if it were a condition instead of a description of an extreme reaction. She never resorted to any crude or slang words. Using God's name was definitely unacceptable to Grandma in any situation.

I embraced the idea of living a less turbulent life style. I had often heard curse words pour from my parents' mouths, especially my dad's. I never felt comfortable with their word battles. I mostly feared the events that sometimes came prior or after, such as fighting, pushing and slamming. That was one of the many other situations, such as never having to carry bruises from belt whippings, being made to wear 'boys' shoes, and being tormented about my size, which I had resolved to never be forced to endure again.

Grandma beckoned me to follow her into what was soon to be one of my favorite places. Her kitchen was neat, clean, and smelled heavenly. We came to a much needed understanding over our meal. She was one to get right to the point. She would often say, "A good understanding makes for long friendships."

"I don't have much money for us to live on," she began. "I only get sixty-five dollars a month from my pension. I'll take care of you the best I can, but we'll have to be saving and work together in this. I know Larson couldn't take care of a young girl like he should. I'd feel better if Edna had told me what she wanted to happen with you. I'll just have to think in my heart that this was what she would have wanted, and we'll go from here. You know I love you and always have. I loved your blessed mother too. Don't ever doubt how much I love my son. If God wants to give you to me, then I guess I'll finally have the little girl I never had."

I understood. A familiar family story was that she'd had seven boys and only one little girl. The stillborn baby girl was said to have looked just like Grandma. One of the baby boys was also still-born. Another boy child, named little Roy, died about age three with colitis, a treatable condition by today's medical standards but deadly in those days. She and Grandpa raised five sons. My dad was next to the oldest.

She continued as though she was thinking out loud: "I always thought God didn't let me have girls, thinking I wouldn't know how to raise them. I guess He feels like I can now, since I'll have you."

"Daddy said he will send us money," I reminded her of his promise to us on the day he left.

"I guess Larson meant well, but no telling how long it will take him to get on his feet, wherever he was going."

It was obvious that neither she nor I believed him, but it sounded good anyway.

"Well, Larson has always had it hard."

Anyone who ever knew Grandma knew she had always been quick to make excuses for Daddy. For that matter, she saw very little wrong that any of her sons did. She didn't want to admit to herself, or to anyone else, that Larson made it hard on himself because of how he chose to live.

"I know you've never had to work in a cotton field, but you'll have to learn to work in one now. I'll get Mrs. Bertram to teach you how it's done. I'll let you keep whatever you can make to buy your school clothes and books." She went on, "I'll expect you to help out. There will be water to pump, clothes to wash, heating oil to be brought in during the winter, and you'll need to pick up after yourself."

I heard every word she said, but the part about the cotton field, and keeping the money I made was what I heard the loudest. I wouldn't have to wear boy's shoes ever again. I could buy myself a pair of real girl shoes!

After dinner we began the task of sorting and placing my belongings. The pile on the porch looked enormous until I realized that everything I could call mine, along with a few of my mother's cherished treasures could be piled in a heap on one end of a small porch.

There were two full size beds in Grandma's bedroom but only one closet. There was however, a long narrow room or space approximately eight foot by sixteen foot between her bedroom and the porch where my pile had been dumped. That space was the former porch, crudely boxed in by Grandpa, for storing canned foods, extra blankets, quilts and such. It was also referred to as a breezeway between Grandma's bedroom and the front porch, the emphasis being on the word *breeze*. The room had no insulation whatsoever. It worked well for storage, and by the time we finished, a small four foot by four foot portion on one end of it, would also work as my closet.

No Southern house was complete without a porch. Grandma's house had two, a front and a back porch. Porches were gathering places, barriers for the blowing rains and home to various potted porch flowers. The ladies of Silver Leaf practically made a competition of adorning their porches with flowers. Grandma was no exception. A strong twine was tightly strung perpendicular on one end of her front porch for climbing morning glories. Miniature rose bushes bloomed on each side of the other end. Recycled coffee cans displaying a variety of petunias and marigolds banked each post.

Her yard, along with all of her neighbor's yards, was clean and well groomed. She went so far as to sweep the bare spots, where grass wouldn't grow, with a broom kept only for that purpose. She took pride in everything, big or small.

Her front porch was mostly for looks. If there was ever a knock on the front porch door, you could bet it was a stranger. Everyone—stranger or not—would be greeted with a beautiful view of porch flowers.

The back porch was the main porch. It was home to the water pump, washing machine, drain tubs, and—the porch swing. All visitors gathered there. It was also the nearest path to the kitchen, which was the central area of her home. Of course, even a greater array of porch flowers found residence on the back porch.

Once my closet was created, we arranged the jars and bedding and made a place for Mama's trunk. A make-shift wall was provided by two old army blankets that were strung over a wire, secured by two tightly driven over-sized nails. The blankets conveniently opened in the middle for easy access.

We worked the entire afternoon constructing a closet for me and clearing the pile from the front porch. In fact, neither of us realized how late it had gotten until Grandma announced, "I'm tired and my dinner has worn off. If it's okay with you, I think we'll just glean for supper."

I followed her to the kitchen and was clueless as what new meal she had planned for us.

"We can have a little dab of this and a little dab of

that," she was saying while transferring bowls of leftovers from her refrigerator to the table.

"Okay, but where is the glean?" I asked, while searching for an unfamiliar dish of something.

"Have you never heard the word glean before?" She asked, partly amused and partly disturbed. "Glean is a Biblical word for gathering the leftovers, as Ruth did from the field belonging to Boaz."

It didn't take her long to see I had no idea of who Ruth was nor knew anything about Boaz and his field. Her work was truly cut out for her.

Explanations were not important at that point. My first bite of her fried chicken confirmed it to be as tasty as when it was fresh out of her frying pan. Also, by the time she presented all the bowls of leftovers, we had a table full of choices from which to glean after all.

As we ate our meal, she told me the beautiful Bible story of Ruth, Naomi and Boaz. I had never known there were love stories in the Bible. The bits and pieces of the Bible that I had been told were all about dos, don'ts, and thunderous commands by an angry God, most of the time. Mama simply had told me that He was always watching me and He was not proud of us if we're bad and was happy with us when we were good. She was quick to tell me that God smiled every time He heard me sing. She always said my voice was a gift from God, and it made me feel special to think He loved me enough to give me a gift. That was pretty much the extent of my Bible knowledge. After that gleaning conversation, Grandma said I had a lot to learn and she planned to see that I did.

Chapter Four

The Cotton Patch

TRANSITIONING FROM A child not expected to pick up her own socks and underwear to one who was now expected to chop and pick cotton was a rude awakening. Living with Grandma had presented a list of chores with my name next to them that would reach from her back porch to the cotton field.

She was constantly saying, "You and I are a team." In Grandma's vernacular, "a team was liken' to two mules, both pulling the yoke and both pulling it in the same direction."

First of all I had no idea what a yoke on a mule looked like and up until then, the only yolk I had ever been familiar with was attached to an egg.

Watching Grandma going about her daily routine revealed her as a hard and very orderly worker. That was God's way of doing things, and she could quote you Scripture to prove it. There was not a lazy bone in her body, and she didn't expect to see one in anyone else's either—especially mine.

After a walk to the Big Store in Muddy Ox a few

days prior, I had four long sleeved work shirts, two pair of jeans, a good pair of work gloves, and at my request, a cheap pair of white tennis shoes. We bought it with most of the thirty dollars that Daddy had left with us that he said was to help with the added expense of me. There was no telling, when or if, we'd see any more money out of Daddy, so we held tightly to the rest.

The smell of breakfast beckoned from the kitchen as I dressed for my first day of cotton chopping. Judging from the pan of fresh biscuits she pulled from the oven as I sat down to the table, Grandma must have gotten up an hour or more before she woke me. She decided to give me some last minute details and instructions while I was eating breakfast.

"Now, I'll take care of all the home duties while you're working in the field. Your duty will be to learn to be a field hand. Emerald Bertram is one of the best and toughest field bosses in these parts but you'll know how to do the job right when she gets through with you."

"Well, at least I will be with Tara, Melly Ann and Scarlett out there in the patch." I was searching for a possible bright side to the ordeal.

"I know you're looking forward to being with the McCrady girls but I'm warning you right now, Emmy will expect you to work while you're there in the field, and you can play later. She won't be mean but getting her cotton patch chopped is going to be first and foremost on her mind. You girls can do a little talking, but you'll need to keep working while you're doing it."

Grandma noticed that I wasn't eating with my usual

enthusiasm. Although everything tasted as good as usual, I had never rolled out of bed that early and gone straight to the breakfast table before.

"I can see you aren't used to eating this early, but you'll be glad you did around ten o'clock. It takes a good breakfast to keep you going 'til noon. These people who say they can't eat when they first get up just haven't ever worked in a cotton field before. If they had, they'd change their minds."

I continued my meal as she continued her last minute prompting.

"You be careful to wear your bonnet out there in the patch. It isn't proper for a lady to have her face all sunburned." I had heard her working far past her bedtime putting the finishing touches on a new sunbonnet for me. It was hanging on my chair post so I wouldn't forget it before I left.

"I had Mr. Simpson from next door to file a good sharp edge on your hoe. It'll have to be sharp to cut through all the Johnson grass and cockleburs. I want to warn you though; it can cut through you too if you're not careful."

The mere thought of having to 'cripple' up and down the rows with a sliced leg gave me cause to want to be extra careful.

"What's a cocklebur?" I wondered, never having heard of one before.

"Right now, they're just little weeds like the rest of the weeds you'll be cutting down. If they're not chopped down though, they become bushes full of seeds that turn into prickly burs that stick to everything they touch. They're nearly impossible to get out of your hair if they get tangled up in it. I've had to cut them out of my hair with scissors before. You can run into a bush of them before you know it, while picking with your head down and not paying attention. Cut down every one you see now, so you won't have to worry with them come picking time."

I'd never heard of cockleburs before, but hearing Grandma warning me about them made me wonder what else was out there that she forgot to tell me about.

"Meryl, learning field work isn't going to be easy, you being a city child. It's hard enough for those raised up around it. But don't worry, hard work never killed anyone." I decided to take that as a promise.

"If hard work could kill a body, I'd already be dead," she added. "I used to not only do all the housework but had to hit the field every day with your Grandpa Omar and the boys too."

Her boys were Frank, the oldest; Larson, my dad; Duncan; Braydon; and baby Paul.

"I pulled 'Paulie' down the cotton row, on top of my sack, so I could nurse him when he was hungry. When he was old enough, I had to leave him on a blanket in the shade of the cotton wagon, and Bray was allowed to stay and watch after him," she offered.

I smiled to hear her refer to my big robust uncle as 'Paulie,' but that was what the whole family called him when he was a baby.

"How old was Uncle Bray then?"

"He was about seven years old. He was good with Paulie, though, even if he was only a child himself. All of the older boys were very protective of their baby brother.

Omar would let me stay home on Saturday mornings with the baby to do the washing. Frank and Larson got the kettle of water heating on a fire heap while I fixed breakfast. I got started with the washing as soon as they all left for the field so I could get it done and we'd have clean clothes to wear to town when they got home at dinner time. Washing shirts and overalls for Omar and five boys by hand on a wash board took a lot of time and elbow-grease for sure."

"Didn't Grandpa let Uncle Bray stay home to help you with the baby on Saturdays?"

"No, he expected each of them to get as much cotton as they could. Bray had to grab a sack and work right along with the others. That's what I meant about hard work killing someone. Why, we'd all be dead if it did."

"I bet Daddy picked the most cotton since he was always so strong," I concluded.

"Well, Larson never took to the cotton patch so much like the others did. He somehow found ways of doing as little as he could get by with when it came to field work. As soon as he could, he learned to drive a tractor and to repair one when it broke down. It was Duncan who always picked the most cotton. He'd sometimes get nearly six hundred pounds a day. That was almost twice as much as the others."

"Did he get paid twice as much?"

"No, Dunk just earned the title of being the best."

"That wasn't fair," I decided.

"Meryl, times were much harder then than they are even now. It took every penny all of us could make just to keep food on the table and to live. Omar gave them all a quarter when we got to town, and they were glad to get it. He'd give me one too, just as he gave the boys," she said quietly.

"A quarter was all you got? Grandpa wasn't very generous, considering you were his wife and all the work you did."

"Well, there was one time that I asked for an extra nickel, but he wouldn't give it to me. A street vendor was selling grab-bags. Being curious about what was in them, I thought I just had to have one. I was embarrassed and cried, when Omar refused to give me that nickel. I never did get to have one of those bags or ever find out what was in them."

"That was mean of Grandpa," I spouted.

"Oh well, I didn't *need* a bag. I just *wanted* one. Omar knew we couldn't afford to waste money on such things as that."

Grandma was being her usual self, by making allowances for Grandpa, as she did so often for Daddy. However, for me, her allowances failed to erase the large black mark that ran across Grandpa's image.

Hearing of how Grandma and her boys worked so hard and only got quarters for their paydays, I felt better about being thrown into the work force if I was being allowed to keep all my earnings.

"I have no idea what is lying ahead of you, Meryl. Your path will be possible, just not easy—especially down a cotton row," she said, handing me my dinner sack and bonnet while following me out of the kitchen.

I shouldered my hoe and was off. Grandma was standing on the porch in the dimness of early morning as I left for my first day's work. I rolled her stories and warnings over in my mind as I waved to her while going to wait for the Bertrams' wagon to take me to the field.

I kicked gravel all the way to the end of the lane, as if symbolically clearing a path to whatever the day would bring. Being taken to what was promised to be the most unimaginably hardest thing I had ever done was somewhat unnerving. I hoped that the morning sky appearing as though an artist had slashed streaks of crimson and purple across his canvas in anger wasn't setting the stage for the remainder of the day.

Then slowly a hint of daylight pushed through the heavy hues and lifted the sun-laced clouds, offering a sense of peace. A slight breeze carried a flowery fragrance and a promise of spring.

Despite my sleepy eyes, my mind was filled with wonder. I had no inkling of what awaited me in the hours to come, but I was, nonetheless, excited about it.

Upon reaching the end of the lane, I heard the Bertrams' temperamental tractor as it sputtered and spit from pulling the cotton wagon that was to take me to my first cotton patch. I wasn't familiar with tractors at all, but being the daughter of a superior shade-tree mechanic I could tell this one had some major mechanical issues. It bucked, snorted, and groaned all the way to the field. Since I had never ridden a cotton wagon before, that alone was an adventure. Being with my friends—Tara, Melly Ann, and Scarlett—only made it better.

They, who were usually babbling like magpies and full of fun and laughter, were notably quiet that morning. It didn't take long to discover that my day was going to be anything but fun. It was going to be about something I knew very little about: work...hard work!

Chapter Five

The Whirlwind Experience

EMERALD 'EMMY' BERTRAM was a short, stocky little woman who was known for her bluntness. The first thing I noticed about her, other than her sharp tongue, was her gold tooth. Having never seen anyone with a gold tooth before, I found it nearly impossible to ignore how it sparked as she talked. If the sun hit it just right, it would glisten to compliment her small, round, blue eyes. She could be quite pleasant if she wanted to be. However, pleasant was not a good description of her in her cotton patch.

"Meryl Jean Strom." she addressed me in her cutting, high-pitched voice.

"What in the world do you mean?"

Tara Gayle, the younger of the McCrady sisters, corrected her by saying, "Jean, Grandma, we call her Jean." Mrs. Bertram gave her a look that said she really didn't care what I was called.

Something must have been seriously wrong for her to use my entire name. I hadn't noticed that she had been following me down my row for quite a while. I pushed my bonnet back to see what she wanted.

"What is it, Mrs. Bertram?"

Thinking I had been doing pretty well gave way to an instant state of confusion. She had taught me how to skillfully take the point of the hoe and cut out the unwanted weeds and grass from around the cotton plant and then carefully pull the dirt up around it in just a few quick swipes. I was pretty pleased with myself and had no idea what she was not happy with.

"Look at this. You have cut down all the cotton on this row so far and left all wild morning glories." Her drawn little mouth spat out the words. Her face was a bright red, making her tiny, round eyes an even more brilliant shade of blue. "I know cotton and morning glories looked a little alike, but I thought I showed you the difference. This row will have to be re-planted. It is not going to have a stalk of cotton on it at all."

My inexperienced eyes had to look very closely to see the difference between cotton and a morning glory plant. It was plain to see what she was upset with and rightly so; there was no market for morning glories. Quick witted and with a child-like innocence, I responded, "Well, at least, I'll have the prettiest row in the field when they bloom."

She almost gave in to a smile but caught herself. She was not used to humorous comebacks when she chastised a new field-hand. Her lips tightened again as she retorted. "Let's not make light of this, girl, your grandma sent you to me to make a field hand out of you, not a gardener. Now you get down real close to learn the difference, and let's not let this happen again."

She was still spitting the words and her head was bobbing disgustedly as she stomped off down the field row, leaving me to my assigned investigation. Her tone sounded a little bit softer, probably due to my previous response. She repeated from a distance that she never wanted that to happen again.

It never did happen again. If it had, I knew I would be dealing with her and Grandma too. Grandma was not a harsh person but she had a way about her that made everyone, especially me, want to be in her good graces. Somehow, I always felt worse to think I might have disappointed her than it actually made her feel to be disappointed. I believed it was because she didn't only talk about it, but truly did try to be fair and live by the Bible's golden rule: "do onto others, as you would have them do onto you." People just didn't or couldn't feel good about it if they knew they hadn't done right by Grandma.

She possessed an integrity and classiness that couldn't be bought. It would have been hard to find anyone who didn't have a deep admiration and unwavering respect for her. I found myself spending the rest of my life trying to emulate her.

Although it seemed much longer, we'd been chopping for only two hours. Waves of heat, caused by the scorching sun, flowed across the field. My bonnet worked well for keeping the sun from my face, but it didn't allow me to feel any breeze, if there'd been one. My feet burned from the baking ground beneath them, and my shoulders ached from continuously swinging the hoe. Despite the gloves, there was a small blister rising between my thumb and forefinger. My tender hands that had never experienced work before were not standing up to the challenge very well. I was already in trouble. It was still four hours before noon, and all I could think about was washing my face in a pan of cold water and resting in the swing on Grandma's back porch. While stopping to examine my blister, I heard Tara yell in excitement.

"Jean, look over there!" She was pointing to a whirlwind that was only a few rows over from me. "Push back your bonnet. It's headed your way," she instructed.

Whirlwinds, also called dust-devils, were common occurrences out in the hot, flat, cotton fields. My whirlwind didn't last long, but it cooled me off a bit and dried my sweating face. Anything that offered relief from the parching, hot sun out in the cotton field was appreciated. I had never been in the midst of a whirlwind before, but from then on, I made it a practice to look long and hard for one that might be headed my direction. I was later to learn there were many kinds of whirlwinds. Some refreshed you; some almost sucked the life out of you.

"Let's get moving now." The watchful eye of Mrs. Bertram was always present. When she saw me lagging behind, she chopped a strip ahead so I could skip to the next spot and catch up again. It was something on the order of hop-scotch. She had already caught me up three times, and it was plain to see she didn't want to continue doing it. I was trying to keep up with her granddaughters, but they had been at this field work for a while and knew how it was done.

"Grandma Bertram, I have to go to the bathroom," announced Melly Ann, the middle sister. This meant her grandmother would be chopping her row while she was gone. It also meant I was on my own to stay up with the others. There were no toilets in the field; so Melly would have to walk a long way to find a thicket dense enough to hide behind.

"Go on Melly Ann. Get over there and back as soon as you can so I won't be tied to your row very long," Mrs. Betram didn't deny her bathroom privileges, but she was well aware of Melly's antics.

"I will," Melly promised as she walked away, but took her sweet time getting to the thicket.

That was a good plan on Melly's part for getting a little break. The longer it took her to find a thicket, the longer her break. Melly was an expert at that. She was always having to go to the bathroom or was too hot and she needed a splash of water on her face. She complained her hoe was dull and needed sharpening, or her shoe was untied. She used whatever she could come up with to get her temporarily away from her hoe and the field.

The sharp metal of my hoe rang as it sliced through the dirt. The sound of many hoes in the hands of the skillful workers, created a rhythm that could almost be compared to a primitive kind of music. At least that was how it sounded to me. I had always been able to hear music in things that others couldn't hear. The blowing wind, the swishing of windshield wipers, the thumping of tires on pavement—all had musical rhythms, at least to my ears.

I used to think my musical abilities might have been God's way of compensating for the other areas in which I was not so gifted. My feet were too wide, I was overweight. I had chubby hands with short, little fingers that were even more unattractive and noticeable because of my habit of biting my nails down to the quick until they bled.

The symphony that was playing in my head helped to take my mind off the torturous heat and the pain of my blister. The clanging of the dinner bell interrupted my private concert and rang a different kind of music to my ears when Mrs. Bertram announced, "Let's go to dinner."

Almost in unison, we shouldered our hoes and headed down our cotton rows. The once busy field was soon empty, and the only movement was the dry-weather flies chasing the mosquitoes in hopes of getting their dinner too. The McCrady girls and I headed for the shade of the wagon to eat our stash.

My trio of friends wouldn't have had to work in the field at all, had their mother and grandmother not shared my grandma's opinion of a work ethic. Their dad worked at the General Motors factory in St. Louis, Missouri. He either made the two hundred-plus mile trip home each weekend, or put his check in the mail.

Their mother didn't see the city as a fit place to raise their daughters; so she and their dad agreed for her to live in Silver Leaf with the girls. He lived in an apartment not far from the plant in St. Louis. It might not have worked for some, but it seemed to work for them.

The girls had beautiful clothes, plenty of food in their refrigerator, candy bars in their freezer, and there was always a case of Pepsi Cola sitting on their back porch. They had sandwiches made with store-bought bread and packaged cookies for dinner.

I would have been envious, if I hadn't had a piece of fried, rag bologna on one of Grandma's biscuits. Their sandwich bread paled pitifully in comparison to Grandma's biscuits. To top it off, there was a fried apple pie in my sack. Grandma fried almost everything.

Chapter Six

An Uninvited Visitor

THE DINNER BREAK seemed entirely too short. Once we were back in the field, it didn't take Melly long to request another bathroom break. Mrs. Bertram again began the task of keeping up her row. Melly's row being next to mine meant I would be watched even more closely.

The morning had been sultry, but the afternoon gave an entirely new meaning to the word *hot*. Suddenly, we heard a distress call from Melly as she raced back toward us. We couldn't understand what she was saying, but the pace she was moving was not a normal one for her, especially in the heat of the day.

"Grandma Bertram, come quick! It's awful. There are dead chickens all over the place near the thicket." The horror on Melly's face confirmed she was telling the truth and this was not one her usual exaggerations.

"Chickens," Mrs. Bertram squeaked, "Why would there be a bunch of dead chickens by the thicket? There isn't even a house around here. I got a whiff of something a while back but thought it must be a dead rabbit or something."

"Well, it isn't. It's chickens. They're dead and scattered all over the place!" Melly, nearly out of breath, could barely speak calmly enough to explain the horrifying sight she had just witnessed.

Mr. Simpson, Grandma's next door neighbor and husband to her longest and best friend Katty, overheard and volunteered to go with Mr. Bertram and check things out. They took their hoes in case there was some sort of varmint still lurking around that could have possibly slaughtered the chickens in a way that could have thrown Melly into such a panic. They returned shortly, and both were shaking their head in what looked like disbelief.

"I'm not sure what went on there; if it'd been an animal that killed 'em, some of 'em wuda been eat'n." Mr. Simpson had seen dead animals before, but he insisted he'd never seen such a sight as that.

"Or at least gnawed on," Mr. Bertram agreed their discovery was not normal but more nearly resembled a massacre. "I don't understand it either. Most of their necks weren't even broke," he added.

Still shaking their heads, the two men went back to work, as though the mystery had been solved. I was not convinced.

"Well, Melly Ann, I'm not sure what this is all about, but you nor any of the other girls, are not to go over there to the bathroom or for any other reason, until we find it out."

Mrs. Bertram had a strange, unreadable expression

on her face. I was sure of one thing. She suspected more than she was telling.

By the time six o'clock rolled around, my blister had burst and was burning like fire. I was more than ready to climb on the cotton wagon and head for the house.

Once off the wagon, I shouldered my hoe and dragged my tired, abused feet down the gravel road toward our back porch. The welcome smell of dinner met me halfway. Grandma knew my first day of hard work would leave me exhausted, hot, and hungry.

I took the wash pan out to the pump, for cleaning up the best I could. A bath of some sort would have to come later. Shortly after Grandpa died, Mr. Simpson moved Grandma's pump from the yard to the porch, making drawing water come wash days much easier. Before I realized it, in true southern fashion, I cupped my hand over the mouth of the pump and slurped water like a pro. Tara told me later it was an unwritten law that one could never leave a pump without getting a slurp of good, cold, water. I decided I was well on my way to becoming one of the bunch of them.

We had just sat down at the table when Grandma got up again, walked over and purposefully latched the screen door. It was dusky dark, but looking through the screen, I could see a shadowy figure edging awkwardly toward the porch.

"Evening, Mrs. Strom. Did you see my old coon dog 'round here today?" The ragged, dirty man timidly asked. He brushed an unmanageable lock of his dark, greasy, hair away from his forehead, making his eyes more visible.

He and Grandma evidently knew each other, since he called her by name. Reluctantly, approaching the porch, he glanced past her to spy who was sitting at her kitchen table, but didn't ask. She wasn't about to volunteer any information either.

"No, her voice was sharp." I didn't see any dogs around here today." She kept one hand on the latch and the other around a heavy wooden, window prop that was leaning against the door-facing, just beyond his view.

She was visibly uneasy about this man. She was not in the habit of locking visitors out of her home. Finally, his curiosity got the best of him.

"Got company?" He inquired while trying to peer past her again. His penetrating stare instantly produced a cold chill over my entire body. His piercing eyes scanned me from head to toe, and I felt even dirtier.

Grandma spoke slowly and deliberately, while still keeping her strong grip on the prop. "It's Larson's girl. She's going to live with me now. Her mother died not long ago. You remember Larson, don't you?"

This was where my dad grew up. Here was where the foundation of his reputation was laid. It was evident, by the expression on his face, that this man was familiar with that reputation and the person to whom it belonged. Grandma knew exactly what she was doing. He shuffled his feet, looked down toward the ground, thanked her, and then turned to walk away. Keeping the screen latched, she held securely to the prop until he was out of sight.

"Grandma, why are you so afraid of that man? Who is he?" I could hardly wait for him to go away and her to return to the table so she could tell me what was going on.

"That is Nate McDougal. He lives over on the other side of Number Eight Ditch. He is not a nice man. Meryl, if you ever see him out, stay away from him. Never carry on a conversation with him, and for sure, never let him in the house." There was indisputable fear in her eyes.

"What's wrong with him? He gives me the creeps." At that point, I felt the need to go wash my hands and face again, but was afraid to go out on the porch. He might still be out there somewhere. I saw him walk away, but he left an eerie presence I couldn't shake.

"He just isn't right. He's been in and out of trouble his entire life. He can't work. No one trusts him enough to give him a job. He doesn't think like normal people. I feel so sorry for his poor mother. Why, that poor thing can't even keep a good brood of chickens for him." Grandma said this as though it was just a normal statement. It wasn't for me.

"Chickens, why can't she have chickens because of him?" I wanted to know, but something told me that I really might not want to ask.

"Meryl, you're young, but you're at an age that you should know certain facts. I know that Edna and Larson never kept too many things from you, even if you were a child. Well, you're a young lady now, and you need to know about people like this Nate McDougal. I love his mother. She is a long time friend of mine, but Nate is a sick man. Some men are just like that. They're like animals. They can't control themselves." Her voice and hands were trembling by now.

"Grandma, what did he do to his mother's chickens?" By this time, I had to know and I wanted her to get on with it.

"Well, Meryl, when a man doesn't have a woman for what comes natural for men and women, do you know what I mean?" I nodded too stunned to actually speak. She continued, "Well, he is so sick, he…he tries to molest his mother's chickens. Sick men like him don't care where they get their pleasures. That's why you should never go near or talk to him." She spouted it all out as quickly as if she was running downhill and couldn't stop.

I maybe knew what she was talking about, I thought. My mother had told me the facts of life, but didn't go into a lot of details.

At that point, food was the last thing on my mind. What a mental picture my grandma painted for me! I was not sure how long we sat in silence, while I rolled that picture over in my mind. I had many questions, but I was embarrassed and too scared of her answers to ask.

Little did I know at the time, but I was safe. She didn't talk openly about those things very well. It was odd to be having a conversation such as that with my elderly grandmother. We girls usually talked about sex and stuff in secret. It was obvious she wasn't comfortable sharing such vivid information with me either.

Finally, we began eating again. I was just about to cut into another biscuit when it hit me.

"Grandma," I shouted! This was the first word either of us had said since the Nate McDougal discussion. I shouted her name so sharply, she dropped her fork.

"Melly found a bunch of dead chickens today behind the thicket by the field when she left to go to the bathroom. Do you think that Nate McDougal man had anything to do with them? Mr. Simpson saw them too. He said their necks weren't even broken and it wasn't clear to him what killed them."

Before she could answer, we heard footsteps on the porch. "Mrs. Strom!" exclaimed Kateline Simpson in her usual booming voice. Her daughter Sadie followed closely behind.

Odd as it was, although Kateline Simpson had been Grandma's dearest and best friend for over forty years, she still called her 'Mrs. Strom.' I guessed it was an old Southern tradition of respect, since Grandma was a few years older. Grandma called her 'Katty,' pronounced as *cat-tee*. I was instructed to call her Miss Katty.

To tell you the truth, if anyone ever did call her Mrs. Simpson, she wouldn't realize they were talking to her. She was just Katty. Sadie called her Mama Katty. Now, Mr. Simpson called her 'Kat.' I, along with almost everyone who knew her, thought it was short for *wild-Kat*.

Miss Katty pulled on the screen with such force, it

was a wonder she hadn't pulled it off its hinges. She was extremely strong for her age and size. Some believed it was because her twin sister, Adeline, died at birth, giving Miss Katty the strength of two. Grandma said it was because she had worked like a mule her whole life. Miss Katty sure plowed into our kitchen like a mule after I unlatched the screen door.

Sadie was right on her heels. She was ten years old but was still undeniably attached to her mother and extremely spoiled. Simp and Katty's love for their little girl blinded their good sense when it came to discipline. Sadie ruled whatever situation she was in. She was her mother's shadow. You saw Katty. You saw Sadie. It was as though there was an invisible leash attached to them. Truth be known, if there had been a leash, you would have been hard-pressed to know who was holding it, Sadie or her mother.

They both pushed into the kitchen past me as I found my chair. "Mrs. Strom, was that Nate McDougal we saw walking through your yard just now? Simp said it looked like him. I don't like that man. Did you hear what Simp saw today near the field? Have you warned Meryl Jean about him?

Miss Katty took a breath and Grandma offered her and Sadie chairs. Sadie was usually glad to come and see us, but that night she was tired and had other things on her mind.

"No, I can't stay, Simp's waiting and I still need to wash Sadie's feet and get her ready for bed."

Washing Sadie's feet was such an ordeal because she

went barefoot most of the time. She didn't like wearing shoes; so she was not made to wear them. Since they didn't have a bathtub or running water, washing her feet meant pumping the water, heating it on the stove, soaking, and then scrubbing them. Sadie only had to sit there while Miss Katty did the scrubbing.

"Yes," it was Nate McDougal. He was looking for his coon dog. I am not happy either, about him coming around. I don't understand. He's never been here at all for anything, not even with his mother when she came to visit. And yes, I've been talking to Meryl about him. When he saw her here, I let him know real quick that she was Larson's daughter."

Grandma and Katty both began nodding their heads in an up and down motion, as though they shared an unspoken mutual understanding about something.

"Yes...well," Miss Katty continued. "Simp went to look, after one of the McCrady girls found a pile of dead chickens near the field today. Simp said they were all layin' there dead with no sign of how they'd been killed. He said it looked real suspicious."

They did that little nodding of the head thing again. "Meryl was just telling me about that before you all came."

All eyes were directed toward me, so to follow Grandma's lead, I continued what I was saying before Miss Katty attacked our screen door.

"Melly found them when she went to the bathroom. She ran back to tell Mrs. Bertram. Then, Mr. Simpson and Mr. Bertram went to see them. That is really all I know."

I no sooner got the words out before Mrs. Walby knocked on the door. It had been left unlatched when Miss Katty and Sadie arrived, so Grandma bade her come on in.

"Mrs. Strom." Effie Walby was another one of Grandma's neighbors and a sister to Mrs. Bertram. Strange as it was, she also had a gold tooth. After living for thirteen years and never having seen even one person with a gold tooth, suddenly in the same day, I had seen two.

"I just wanted to come over and let you know that we think it looks like Nate McDougal is at it again. Jake heard up at the Big Store that those chickens they found today had been violated in the worst way."

Her eyes grew large as she, Grandma, and Miss Katty all three did the nodding thing together.

"I tell you, that man needs to be put away. I just don't think it's safe to have him freely walking around. It really isn't safe for you and this little girl here by yourselves."

Effie had the sweetest voice that almost sang as she talked but that night, her voice contained a flat note of fear.

"Effie, I've lived by myself since Omar died. I haven't had a problem yet. Now, I have Meryl. I think we'll be okay. Larson won't be gone forever. He'll be back around here before long. I let Nate know that Meryl is Larson's daughter."

After I heard Grandma say that, I felt as though that

was one time it was a good thing to be the daughter of Larson Strom.

"Well, just the same, you lock your doors and windows and keep something handy to defend yourself with if you need to. You know that Jake and me are not far away." Effie reassured Grandma, while reaching for the door.

"Simp and me are just next door, Mrs. Strom." Katty's words were for Effie's ears more than Grandma's. Jake and Simp would come running to tackle any offender, as Grandma well knew. She also suspected an offender might dread even more the prospect of being tackled by her friend, Katty Simpson.

Miss Katty and Sadie lingered a few minutes after Mrs. Walby left. Sadie was getting tired of not being the topic of conversation and began tugging at her mother, saying "Mama Katty, I want to go home. I'm tired and want to go home now." She was probably more than ready for her promised foot-washing.

"Mrs. Strom," Miss Katty began in a somewhat softer voice than usual. "You don't need to call on Jake Walby. If you need anything, you can yell for us. We are right next door, practically in your yard. Simp and me will hear you."

Now, John Simpson might have heard us call for help, but Miss Katty couldn't hear thunder if her hearing-aid was turned off. Everyone assumed that was why she spoke so loudly. She couldn't hear, so she decided no one else could either. She didn't realize the magnitude of her voice. My dad jokingly quipped that she was the only person he knew who could step out on her back porch and call for her cats to come home from Number Eight Ditch, a mile away. There might have been a little exaggeration there, but not much.

I was not sure if it was jealousy or honor related to friendship, but Miss Katty wanted her and Simp to be the ones who rescued us if we ever needed any rescuing.

"Of course, if we have problems, I'll call you and Simp, but I'm really not scared—nor do I think anything is going to happen."

Miss Katty felt a little more at ease; so she and Sadie left to wash Sadie's feet and make her ready for bed.

We finally got to finish our supper, which had gotten cold by now. I was too tired to care much at that point.

"Grandma, did you mean what you said when you told Miss Katty that you were not afraid?" I asked for my own peace of mind.

"I… don't think we have anything to worry about. Now you wash up and let's hit the bed. Five o'clock comes real early. Tomorrow is another field day."

The sound of her voice put a big kink into that *at ease feeling* I was reaching for. Nonetheless, I went through the motions of my sponge bath and fell into bed.

Chapter Seven

Sex Talk in the Wagon

SLEEP WAS A far reach at first. Miss Katty's shrill voice was still pounding in my head. The mental picture of what that horrible man must have done to those poor chickens would not go away. Most of all, a chill ran through my entire body as I remembered the roaming eyes of Nate McDougal. That memory—added to the ache in my arms and back—made for a very restless night.

The next morning, every bone in my body cried out. My blister had hardened and the skin cracked open with each movement of my hand. My feet were swollen so big I could hardly wiggle them into my tennis shoes. I was just thirteen years old. Hard work wasn't supposed to make me feel like that. I had forgotten that it was the first hard work I had ever done in my entire life. Had it not been for the smell of bacon frying and the heavenly aroma of freshly baked biscuits coming from the kitchen, I was not sure I could have forced myself to move.

GRANDMA WAS BUSY with breakfast and already had my dinner packed into an empty sandwich bread bag. She solicited them from some of the neighbors, since store bought bread was a rarity for us. She would say, "Those empty bread bags are the handiest little things there ever was."

That woman never threw anything away. Coffee cans especially had a great number of uses, such as flower pots, storage, and night buckets, as to not have to take a run to the toilet after dark. Food, by all means, was not wasted. Leftover beans became fried bean cakes or bean dumplings; yesterday's mashed potatoes were the next day's fried potato fritters. Remaining biscuit dough was used to concoct what she called "clabber." Clabber was created by mixing the dough with a little buttermilk and water in a special, heavy glass jar, covered with a cheesecloth, weighted down with a saucer and kept in the refrigerator for several days until it clabbered or soured, similar to the consistency of buttermilk.

Biscuit making was always an ordeal to watch. Grandma sifted a mound of flour into a large crockery bowl. Using the back of her hand, she hewed out a hole in the middle of it. She then, poured the clabber, water, melted lard, and a pinch of sugar to make the biscuits brown evenly. There was no need for any other ingredients. Self-rising, was her flour of choice.

With her right hand, she raked a small amount of flour from the side of the crock and carefully worked it into the clabber mixture while constantly turning the bowl with her left hand. The process was completed when the dough was shaped into a perfect ball. Flouring both hands, she lifted the dough-ball out of the crock onto the center of a square, wooden cutting board that had been generously dusted with flour. Patting the dough-ball to a desired thickness, she precisely cut each biscuit. After greasing both sides, she then placed them in rows, into a baking pan that had also been ...very well greased. Grandma didn't hold back when it came to greasing things. She would often say, "a little grease is good for your system to keep you regular." After about twenty-five or thirty minutes in a hot oven, out popped some of the best tasting biscuits one could ever hope to slap a pat of butter on.

There was always a bowl of "clabber" brewing in the refrigerator. I figured that her clabber was the secret ingredient that set her biscuits apart from everyone else's.

Any leftover cornbread crumbs or other food, after it had been warmed up past *fit to eat*, got thrown into the chicken pen.

Chickens and a little garden were all we tried to manage. We couldn't afford to feed livestock, and besides we didn't have space for them on our small corner lot. She said chickens more than paid for themselves in eggs and meat. Over the years, I found that to be satisfyingly true.

Dinner in my bread sack and a poultice that Grandma had made *out of...who knew what* on my blister, I was waiting at the corner of the lane for my ride. To hold the poultice in place, I was sporting a tighter pair of gloves. Mr. Bertram would need to sharpen my hoe as soon as we got to the field. It didn't take Johnson grass and gumbo clods very long to dull a hoe.

Smoke was barreling from the exhaust stack of the tractor and the gears were grinding as Mr. Bertram shifted into low for pulling the wagon over the ruts and holes in the road.

As badly as I dreaded the field again, I could hardly wait to get there, to tell Melly and her sisters about our visitors the previous night. The McCrady girls could be heard talking and teasing one another, long before I saw the wagon. One sound of Mrs. Bertram's stern voice brought silence, except for the wagon wheels crunching the gravel road and the putt-putt of the tractor motor. I climbed aboard and took my place. My plan was not to say anything to the girls until the ears of all of the adults were out of range. The plan was spoiled as soon as Tara Gayle blurted out her news, in front of her grandmother, God, and everyone else in the wagon.

"Jean, did you hear about the chickens? It was Nate McDougal. He killed the chickens by...."

Tara was quickly interrupted by Mrs. Bertram. "Now, Tara Gayle, hush. You girls shouldn't be repeating things you hear your mother and me talking about."

Tara couldn't keep quiet if it killed her. She leaned

over next to me and continued in a loud whisper, "He had sex with the chickens."

Try as anyone might, there was no shutting up Tara. The other two girls chimed in. Mrs. Bertram turned her back to us and pretended not to hear the conversation.

"I heard," I added, after I was able to wedge in.

"Your Aunt Effie came over to our house last night during supper and told Grandma. You know what else? Nate McDougal came in our yard." I was so glad I could tell them something they didn't already know.

"He did—he came to your house?" Melly's eyes were big with surprise.

"Well," I continued, "Grandma never let him in, and she would have hit him with the window stick if he had tried to come in, but he didn't. He said he was looking for his dog."

"His dog," Mr. Bertram joined in at that point. "His dog got ran over by Sid Carson's car last week," he continued.

Mrs. Bertram addressed her husband as if they are the only two in the wagon at that time.

"Asa, you need to go let Mrs. Strom know about that dog. I am sure Nate is up to no good, pretending to be looking for a dog that is already dead."

That was not just a mere suggestion to her husband; it was more in the way of a direct order. The field-boss in Mrs. Bertram was calling the shots there in the wagon too. As far as she was concerned, it was time to take aim and Nate McDougal was the target.

I was anxious to reach the field, where I hoped I

could get the girls away from everyone to find out just how much they knew about someone having sex with a chicken. I was only thirteen. I didn't know a whole lot about adults having sex with one another. I was sure my mother would have gotten around to explaining everything eventually. She had always been good to answer any questions I had. Until now, I didn't have the right ones to ask. I couldn't conceive talking to Grandma about such things. I sure hoped the girls knew it all.

Finally, I got my chance. "Tara, just how does a man…you know, with a chicken?" I whispered.

"Jean, you're so silly. Why they," Tara was just about to get to the very details when Miss Katty's shrill voice broke in.

"Simp, Simp." Everyone in the field heard her yelling for Mr. Simpson. Dropping his hoe, he met her midway down the row.

"Simp, Sadie just told me that Nate McDougal tried to get her to go with him to look for his dog the other day. Simp, I don't want him anywhere around our Sadie." Miss Katty was so upset that she was spitting each angry word, much like Mrs. Bertram was the day I chopped down my row of cotton and left the morning glories.

That was when I made matters even worse. "Mr. Bertram told us this morning that Nate's dog got ran over by Mr. Carson's car last week."

Horror struck their faces upon hearing that bit of information.

"I'll kill him, if he touches Sadie." Simp growled.

"I'll kill him too," Miss Katty spat again. "He's an evil, evil man!"

"It's plain to see that we all should keep our eyes and ears open concerning Nate McDougal. If anything else happens, we need to get the law on his trail," Mr. Bertram said while trying to keep a civil head in the matter.

Scarlett, the oldest McCrady girl, started sobbing and everyone turned to see what was wrong with her.

"What's the matter, Scar?" Mrs. Bertram asked.

"He scares me. He scared me the other day. I was walking home from school, and I could see him hiding behind trees, following me. I thought he was just being silly, but he isn't silly, Grandma Bertram; he's scary."

Scarlett was then comforted by her grandmother and sisters. Upon hearing that report, Mrs. Bertram addressed her husband in much the same way as earlier that morning in the wagon.

"Asa, I don't like the sound of this. Something must be done."

Asa Bertram was normally a gentle man, but when he heard Scarlett describe how that monster had been trailing her, he immediately had the look of a hardened man of steel. His eyes narrowed, his jaw tightened, and the whole civil-headed attitude he was trying to have with John and Katty Simpson earlier was gone. His fist clenched the hoe handle so tightly that I expected to see finger prints embedded into it when he released his grip.

Mrs. Bertram edged a little closer and calmly said,

"Now, Asa, I just meant we can't sit back and wait for something else to happen. Now's the time we should take this matter to the authorities," she added in a slow and calming tone as she patted his shoulder.

The tension in his face began to ease as he slowly regained his composure. His fingers relaxed their grip on the hoe handle. Relief swept over Mrs. Bertram's face.

Something about that whole episode gave me the impression she had been witness to that reaction from him before. Considering her quick response, it also occurred to me that this was probably a mild reaction compared to what it could have been.

Mr. Bertram invited Mr. Simpson to accompany him to town to file a report. Simp agreed and Miss Katty insisted on tagging along. Sadie would stay under Grandma's watchful eye until their return.

Mrs. Bertram positioned the girls on one side of her and me on the other. She didn't want us talking any more about Nate McDougal, chickens or, for that matter, anything else. Work was all she wanted to see or hear out of any of us. The quietness of the remainder of the day held no comparison to the excitement of the morning.

I was glad it is Friday. Only a half day's work the next day and we could go to town. Saturday trips to town were a big thing in those parts. Kennett, Hayti, Steele, and Caruthersville were all booming little towns that were less than an hour from Muddy Ox. Mr. Simpson and Miss Katty welcomed us to ride to town with them. They usually left the choosing of the town to Sadie, and she usually chose Steele.

Our money supply would normally have been low considering it was the third Saturday of the month, however not that time. Grandma had a few dollars left over from her monthly check, added to the remains of what Daddy gave her, plus, I had the wages from my partial first week's work. It would be my first Saturday and the first time for spending my own hard-earned money. Fridays were a little less gruesome, just thinking about getting to go to town the next day.

It was a quiet wagon ride home. We were all hot, tired and lost in our own thoughts. Discussing the Nate McDougal issue would have to wait for another, more convenient time. Mrs. Bertram did well at keeping us busy and never allowed the opportunity for private conversations.

Grandma was waiting in the porch swing for me. Mr. Simpson and Miss Katty filled her in on the events of the day as they came to gather Sadie. She hoped all would die down now that the case was in the hands of the law. I was glad and ready to think about other things—like going to town, spending my money and buying school stuff. We didn't have any visitors that night. We just ate and enjoyed a little small talk. I fell into bed shortly after my sponge bath. I reminded myself again how happy I was to be forgiven kitchen detail on work nights. I don't think I could have lifted my hands to do one more thing that evening.

Chapter Eight

My Beautiful Girl Shoes

A LOUD CLAP of thunder and the pounding of rain on our tin roof awoke me that Saturday morning. I happily rolled over and snuggled into the sheets. There would be no chopping that day. Chopping cotton during a thunderstorm was just not done.

First of all, it was dangerous. There were several horrifying stories of how hoe blades got struck by lightning. The McCrady girls briefly shared a story of one such tragedy concerning a classmate of theirs who was chopping in the field with her sisters. A storm was approaching, but the field boss calculated its arrival far enough away that the crew might finish out the patch before it got to them. Of course the children in the field saw the storm as an early ending to their day. The younger sister started singing, "*Rain, rain, come this way, me and Patsy want to play.*" As soon as the words left her lips, a lightning bolt came from what seemed to be nowhere. Her blade was struck, killing her instantly where she stood and leaving her distraught family shocked and helpless. From that time on, farmers were very careful to vacate the fields at the first sign of a possible electrical storm.

Second, in addition to the danger, the dirt in those parts was referred to as gumbo. The Indian word meaning *liquid mud* is where Pemiscot County got its name. It is a rich, black soil that became a gummy mud once it got wet. It would stick to our shoes and hoe, and if allowed to harden, was as heavy as concrete. The gumbo soil was good for growing crops but, once wet, became nearly impossible to work in.

My little extra sleep-time was interrupted by Grandma who announced that I needed to get up, eat, and take my Saturday bath so we could leave for town. Simp, Miss Katty, and Sadie wanted to get a jump on the crowd. I was enjoying the added sleep, but getting to go to town earlier and shop longer made getting up all worthwhile.

Knowing we would be pressed for time and not wanting to keep the Simpsons' waiting, Grandma already had a kettle and a big pan of water heating on the stove for my bath. After breakfast, I carried several buckets of pump water to fill the galvanized bathtub waiting for me in the garage, also referred to as the shed and the bathhouse.

The pan of boiling water along with that in the kettle was just barely enough to take the edge off the frigid pump water. After a few minutes, my body temperature adjusted, and how wonderful it felt to become completely submerged in the tub. There was no comparison between my sponge-baths and a relaxing full-body bath.

I wished I could have taken a real bath every night but it was impossible. There wasn't enough time, nor did I have the energy after a long day of work, to get home, eat supper, prepare the water, and then get into bed in time to get enough rest for the next hard day. We worked from six in the morning until six in the evening. The wagon ride home took another hour. Supper was another hour at least. I would have been up until after ten o'clock every night, just trying to take a bath. If I made it to the end of the lane to be picked up by the Bertrams' wagon in time, I'd have had to get up before five each morning. Sponge baths would just have to do, during the week.

Sadie, Grandma, and I piled into the back seat, and we were off to Steele. Sadie had been given two dollars. She loved Steele's five and dime store and would be heading there as soon as she could escape the parked car. I didn't mind where we went. It had been over a month since my dad left. This was the first outing I'd had, other than the trips to the cotton patch. I didn't even mind Sadie's whining…too much.

It didn't take long once we got to town to discover that everyone else had the same idea. The streets of Steele were filled with people. There was excitement in the air. You could hear laughter and see pride on the sunburned faces throughout the crowd. Their weekly trips to town were a welcome reward for their hard weeks' work.

This usually sleepy little place was anything but quiet

on Saturdays. Stores up and down the street had their doors propped open wide for easy access and a cool breeze. The railroad track crossing Main Street was filled with pedestrians. This was not a problem. Everyone knew the train ran only twice daily and was not expected until late evening. We found a parking space near the tracks, and all eagerly piled out of the car, with Sadie leading the pack as Miss Katty struggled to catch up with her.

Mr. Simpson headed for the stockyards. He enjoyed watching the cattle auction even if he wasn't going to be a bidder. He also looked forward to a little *man talk*. Being the only male at his house and ours, he was a little outnumbered.

Grandma and I made our way to the Dollar Store. She had a list to fill; so we made a plan to meet back at the car in two hours. I had twelve dollars for my two days' labor. I would have been three dollars richer, had the storm not rained us out, but I was happy to have three dollars less and not have to face the field that day. The Dollar Store had it all, but shoes were what I had on my mind. The style at that time was pointed toes. I hoped to find a pair that I could squeeze my wide feet into.

I wouldn't allow my eyes to even glance toward the men's shoe department while searching for the ladies' shoes. With a little luck, I would be crossing my first *never—no more* boy's shoes—off my list. That felt good.

MR. SIMPSON WAS leaning against the car, with his arms and ankles crossed, watching the sea of people sweep from one side of the street to the other. As we approached, he peered past us for signs of his wife and daughter. Based on the length of time they had been gone, he figured Sadie was still trying to con Kat out of one last purchase that she was sure she couldn't live without. His wife was a pushover for their daughter and found it nearly impossible to tell her no. Thinking about it, I wasn't sure Sadie even knew the definition of the word no. Mr. Simpson couldn't afford to be too critical; he was no better at discipline himself.

The car was very warm, but Grandma's and my feet were tired, so we climbed into the back seat anyway. All of the windows were down, and there was a slight breeze blowing through, making it a little more bearable. Getting off our feet was worth tolerating the heat as long as Miss Katty and Sadie didn't take much longer.

We started going through our packages, sharing our finds while we were waiting. Grandma was too practical to fall prey to the weakness of impulse buying, so she hadn't bought very much. Sticking to necessities, she got a large box of stick matches for lighting the stove, a new piece of cheesecloth to cover her clabber, and a bar of bath soap. Soap got used up a little faster, now that there were two of us taking baths. She also had something I'd never seen before. It was in a square, green tin can. She removed the lid, and immediately the smell of it filled the car.

"Whew, what is that?" I quizzed.

"It's Bag Balm. Farmers use it on cows' udders to keep them from cracking. It works real well on rough hands, and it's good for your feet too. You'll need it now that you are a field hand." The odor lingered long after she closed the tin.

We hadn't noticed Miss Katty and Sadie's arrival until Sadie started to gag and complain about the smell of the Bag Balm no sooner than she got wind of it. The smell cleared once the car began to move. Mine and Grandma's hair was being blown every which way, with all of the car windows being rolled down; but we were glad to give up our hairdos for the cool ride home.

Miss Katty shared the stories about her bargains with her husband, while Sadie played with yet another new doll. She ripped a snap from the doll's dress and had its hair all out of sorts even before we left the streets of Steele. I was thankful she had something to get her mind off the smell from the Bag Balm at least. When Sadie wasn't happy, neither was the pair up front.

Right before we crossed the Number Eight Bridge, leading to Muddy Ox, Sadie opened a little vial of Ben Hur perfume and began to dab it on herself and her doll. If we thought the Bag Balm was strong, the perfume took our breaths!

Grandma said, "Sadie, it smells like a French whorehouse in here." Everyone laughed but Sadie.

"What's a French whorehouse?" she asked, causing

us to laugh harder. Sadie forgot the question and Miss Katty was glad. She wasn't prepared for that conversation with her little girl just yet, especially in mixed company. As usual, Mr. Simpson added nothing to the conversation, but couldn't hide the half-smile on his slightly flushed face. I might have been wrong but my mind couldn't place that timid man who, to me, was above reproach, in a whorehouse of any kind.

Once at home, I couldn't hide the excitement of trying on and showing my shoes to Grandma. They were black patent leather with narrow, white stripes across the toes. I had to get a size too big, so they would stretch wide enough, but they worked. She complimented them, and I grinned from ear to ear. I had a pair of real girl shoes, and I had made the money to pay for them myself! In addition, I bought four pairs of underwear, on sale, four for a dollar, a new bra, and a white cotton blouse. I also got a hand mirror for fixing the back of my hair. All that and I still had one dollar and twenty-nine cents left. This was 1959, and prices were more reasonable than today's. Twelve dollars would stretch much farther.

"You want to wear your new shoes to church tomorrow evening? Jake and Effie are always asking me if we want to go." Grandma asked.

"Yes, if you want to." I was glad for any chance to get to wear my new shoes.

Jake Walby had a reputation of fault-finding and grumbling, but with that said, he had a good heart and Grandma clearly loved his wife, Effie.

We would have gone with Miss Katty and Mr. Simpson if they'd attended church anywhere regularly. Their excuse was that Sadie didn't enjoy being confined, so they planned to wait until she was more settled. I guess that excuse was as good as any, though it wasn't nearly good enough for Grandma.

"I can't understand why it is that people find it so hard to go to church but so easy to be up for going almost anywhere else. It worries me that the Simpsons aren't regulars at any church. I know they weren't raised up that way. It also distresses me that they don't find it important to overrule Sadie's will and take her either. I hope they don't wait too much longer before she really gets set in her ways."

Most people who had been around Sadie longer than an hour or two would have argued that child was already *set in her ways.*

"Oh, well, I can't fix them. I'll have to add that to the long list of many other life matters that I can't fix. What I can do is to see that we get to church. After all, God had finally given me a little girl." Grandma's embrace gave me a feeling of being wanted and belonging that replaced the intrusiveness I had felt at being dumped on her porch. For the first time, I felt as though I was at home and not just as a visitor.

OUR FIRST TRIP to Jake and Effie's church was on Sunday evening. I felt so proud to be wearing the new clothes that I'd worked for and bought myself. The last thing I put on was my new shoes. My feet weren't used to being crammed into pointed toes, so I could be in for a little pain until they got broken in. I decided that didn't matter, pain in my feet or pain in my heart. It was a trade-off. I'd rather my feet hurt a little and look like the other girls than be clunking around in boys' shoes. I could handle it. I loved them, pain, pointed toes and all.

We heard the car approaching on the gravel as Jake Walby turned the corner to our house. After greetings and introductions, we were off.

"Mrs. Strom, I hear that Meryl sings." Jake inquired as he had me focused in his rear view mirror.

I'd heard Grandma and Miss Katty speak of him, but I had never met him before. Effie smiled as she turned to me, sitting in the back seat. Her gold tooth glistened as it reflected the late afternoon sun.

"Yes, she has a very pretty voice." Grandma responded. Effie was still turned and smiling.

"Well, maybe she'll honor us tonight. I'll be glad to say something to Bro. Gayle," Effie volunteered.

Jake still had me focused in the mirror, and I was wishing he would pay a little more attention to the road and not me. Hayti was a good forty-five minutes away. If we were going to get there at all, he was going to have to look where he was driving or we could end up in a gumbo bog.

"Why…" Grandma started.

I spoke up and interrupted, "Ok, if the preacher wants me to."

I was tired of them talking about me as though I wasn't even there. I didn't have a scared bone in my body when it came to singing. It didn't matter to me that it was a church I hadn't ever attended before or people I'd never met. Singing to me was like breathing was to most people.

As she suggested, Effie spoke to the preacher and I was asked to sing. Their church services were laid-back and informal, so it was nothing out of the normal for someone to be asked to sing impromptu. Bro Gayle announced, "We have a new young lady in our congregation tonight, and I have been told she is willing to sing a special song for us. What is your name, dear?" he sweetly inquired.

Although I told him loud and clear that my name was Jean, he heard it as Jeannie. This was the beginning of a second new name for me.

"Well, all right, Jeannie, come on up here and sing for us."

After that first song, I was asked to sing every time we attended services. I loved it.

Now, I had two new identities, Jean and Jeannie. Most important, neither of them rhymed with barrel. Grandma still called me Meryl, but that was ok, she was safe.

Chapter Nine

Goats Dogs Kids

I T WAS MONDAY morning again. The dollar and twenty-nine cents, the new clothes, and my long-desired girl shoes were good incentives for dragging myself down the road to catch the Bertram's wagon and head to the field again.

As usual, I hadn't seen the McCrady girls all week-end. They attended the Church of Christ a few miles from town. It wasn't common for them to shop in Steele or any of the other little towns nearby. They had a good car, and their mom either took them to Memphis or ordered their clothes from a catalog. They could use their field money as they chose.

The Nate McDougal episode had quieted down now that everyone was sure he was in the trustworthy hands of the law. I still had a few questions for Tara and the other girls, but those would have to wait.

Before long, I could hear the wagon coming, carrying its load of giggly girls. I was anxious to tell them about my new black patent leather shoes with a little white stripe across the toe.

"They sound cute. I think I saw some like that in a catalog the other day," Melly offered.

"We haven't even started shopping for school yet," said Tara.

I hadn't told anyone, but my shoes were not name-brand. It was doubtful my friends had seen them in their catalog. I don't think they realized how important those shoes were to me. After all, they didn't have foot issues or, for that matter, weight issues either. If I hadn't liked them so much, I think I could have been jealous.

The tractor came to a halt. We jumped off the wagon, shouldered our hoes, and headed for the field. After a nod from Mrs. Bertram, the day began.

The sun was already peeking through the horizon with a steamy promise of what was ahead. The field was surprisingly quiet this morning. All the workers seemed to be in their own little world. It was easy to let ones mind wander where it might, and delve deeply into aimless thoughts. I was happily remembering my shopping adventure from Saturday past. I had a brand new pair of girl shoes, and it didn't matter that they weren't name-brand. I was sure that no one would make fun of me for wearing those shoes to school.

I hadn't chopped very far down the row before my happy shopping memories were invaded by a rank odor and the sound of several bleating goats caged in a make-shift pen across the way. Goats are stinky animals. I knew this first-hand. This stench triggered a rather unpleasant memory for me.

When I was about nine years old, my wheeling,

dealing dad had traded a coon dog for a pair of goats. He planned to raise them for their milk. Believe it or not, the man who didn't practice any other healthy habits boasted about the health benefits of goats' milk. Healthy or not, I didn't like the taste of it.

I never liked the goats either. The male, which was a dark brownish red in color, had big, angry looking horns. I was assigned the job of feeding and watering Old Red and his mate Nanny.

Many times I would walk two steps and Old Red would butt me three more. I was scared to death of him. Despite my tears and protest, Daddy insisted that the big, red, stinky thing was safe. My mother would help me with the dreaded chore when Daddy was not around. She wasn't convinced the goat was not a threat either.

I had a pleasant surprise one day as I arrived home from school. Old Red and Nanny had been blessed with a pair of snow white baby goats. They were irresistibly sweet and cuddly, despite the fact that they too, smelled like goats. I named them Billy and Snowy. They followed me around like little puppies. Being an only child, I was constantly looking for companions. I made pets out of almost every animal Daddy collected.

We always had an unusual mix of animals. Daddy had several prize red and blue tick coonhounds. It was not uncommon for them to have twelve or more puppies with each litter. I made pets of all of them as long as Daddy would allow. I fed them with pet nursing bottles and dressed them in doll clothes until he decided they were old enough to be trained as hunters.

If all of this taught me anything, it was not to get overly attached to any of them. My companionship with them was usually short-lived. Often I would start to play with my puppies, only to find one or two of them missing. I didn't need to ask. Daddy had no qualms about disposing of the runts or down-sizing the puppy count if he deemed it necessary. It was a scene I accidentally walked in on one day and *never* wanted to witness again! While holding the puppies by their feet he slammed their heads up against a post in the pen with one forceful swipe. There was another '*never.*'

Daddy had a full grown boar raccoon that he captured during a hunt, whose sole purpose was to train his dogs. It was a mean thing and rightly so. Daddy tied him in one corner of the dog pen to taunt the trainee dog that was tied in the opposite corner. The hissing raccoon would claw and spit at the dog. The dog in turn would growl and nip back. They were close enough to bite and claw one another but were not close enough that either could be killed. After a few training sessions, the dog and the raccoon hated each other and their scents. Both were a bloody mess after each ordeal. It was a cruel, unconventional way to train a coon dog, but it worked. Heaven help the raccoon that got in the path of Daddy's two prize hunting dogs, Old Blue and Queenie.

The poor old raccoon's purpose ended suddenly one day when Old Blue broke his chain. The well-trained dog, in only a few seconds, ended the coon's dreaded life, which wasn't much of one anyway. Of course, it wasn't long until Daddy captured another, even bigger, meaner, trainer coon to take its place.

With raccoons, goats, many dogs and a stray cat now and then, we practically had a zoo. Because of a lay-off at work, Daddy did his usual thing one morning of barking orders to pack for an extended stay that time, at Grandma's. Of course, we couldn't leave our zoo unattended. We had no choice but take most of them with us. This would have been a dilemma for a lot of people, but Daddy had it all figured out. The car would hold only so many of us; so down-sizing was a necessity.

He killed or sold all of the puppies but four, along with my baby goat, Billy. The new bigger, meaner raccoon would be caged in the trunk and placed under the spare tire. Old Red and Snowy would ride back there too. This left two coon dogs, a nanny goat, four hound puppies and me to ride in the back seat all the way from Illinois to Missouri. The seat cushion was removed and a tool box put in its place for me to sit on. Mama placed a folded blanket over the box so I wouldn't have such a hard seat for the journey.

What would have normally been about a five hour trip, stretched into another hour or so travel-time. Had I known better or felt privileged to do so, I would have complained. But, sadly, it was nothing out of the ordinary to me.

The dogs and Nanny were given several bathroom stops, which Mama and I took advantage of as well. I didn't remember the goats in the trunk ever getting the same privilege. Being confined in the back seat with all those animals for that many hours was the last thing my mother wanted for me. Nonetheless, protesting would have been in vain with a man who had already consumed a half pint of whiskey and was convinced that his way was the only way.

Somewhere about mid-way into our journey, Old Blue and Queenie got into a squabble. Queenie bit Blue's ear and he slung blood all over me and everything else in the back. Daddy stopped to gas up the car and to assess the situation.

A man at the bay beside us glanced toward our car just as I peeped out of the window. Next, old Blue stuck his head up to see what was going on. He stepped on Nanny's foot and she let out a loud bleat and rammed her head against the window too. All this commotion caused the puppies to start barking.

The curious man finally asked my dad, "What do you have in that back seat, Man—dogs, goats, or kids?"

Daddy looked back at him before getting into the car and said, "yes." We sped off, leaving the bewildered onlooker to figure it out for himself.

What a mess we were by the time we got to Grandma's house. Mama had to wash every piece of clothing we had brought. If not covered with blood, it smelled of goat or dog. Daddy let the car sit with the trunk and doors open for an entire day so it would air out as best it could.

Luckily, the three goats were sold to one of Grandma's neighbors. Old Blue finally got to the replacement raccoon just as he did the first one, and that was the end of him. The puppies were given away. Mama and I were thankful our return trip was not as eventful as the first one. There was another *never*. I would *never* have to deal with such travel arrangements as that again!

Comparing the many trips we made from Illinois to Grandma's over the years, I think that one could have been a close second to the last unpleasant and painful one we had made after being uprooted after my mother's death.

THE SHARP PAIN in my hand from the return of the partially healed blister, snapped me back to the present. I had finally chopped down the row far enough to leave behind the offensive smell of goats and the memory they triggered. My hair was dripping with sweat. My throat was thirsty and parched from the sweltering heat. I then spied Mrs. Bertram heading toward us with a water bucket. Unlike the many other times, she was a very welcome sight that day. The water wasn't cold by the time she got to us, but it was wet, and that was better than nothing. Everyone drank from the same dipper. What is thought to be unsanitary by today's standards wasn't given a second thought in a cotton field.

Actually, not everyone drank from the same dipper. The line was drawn when it came to the Mexicans and the black folks sharing the water bucket and dipper in the field. They didn't ever share the same bucket and dipper with each other anywhere at all. Each group had its own water person, bucket and dipper. It was the South in 1959, and it was just understood. Schools, churches and most public places were still segregated. All of us shared the same cotton patch, work challenges, and pay scale but not the same water bucket, dipper or bathrooms.

Working with black folks didn't bother me like it did some of the others. My dad's desire to have a *zoo* and his choice of lifestyle didn't allow us to live within the city limits in Illinois. It also didn't put us in the elite part of town. We had black neighbors who lived up the hill from us. Sometimes, while Daddy was at work, Mama allowed me to play with the children. They were my friends. I was color-blind, as are most children.

I was fascinated by how the black families worked hard, consistently, and thoroughly in the cotton fields. No straggling cotton was ever left strewn on their rows. I never heard them squabble with each other or complain.

I loved to hear their deep, soulful voices as their sweet, rich harmony rang out over the field. Plain and ordinary songs would become songs filled with passion and rhythm. They could sing for me any time they wanted to. I sang along with them sometimes, but of course…on my side of the field.

It was about an hour until noon. I decided because of that refreshing drink of water, I could make it until dinner time. The closer it got to noon, the hotter the sun beat down on us. I was remembering my whirlwind experience that first day and thought, "Lord, where is a whirlwind when I need one?"

Finally, the much welcomed call for dinner came. After we'd eaten our dinners, and the girls and I were lying down under the shade of the wagon for a few more minutes of rest before hitting the field again.

Even though my eyes were closed, I sensed a deeper shadow of shade above me. I opened them to see what I decided must have been the most enormous black woman I had ever seen!

"Kin you tell me wher Mista' Bertram mite be?" she asked.

Melly never spoke, but only pointed toward her grandfather, who was on the other side of the field road.

The gentle giant was carrying a large canteen of water on each shoulder as she shuffled toward Mr. Bertram, who was sharpening hoes underneath a large pecan tree. Pecan and walnut trees had been spared during the original clearing of the land. It was always a bonus to get to work in a field that had them. They offered good, deep shade in the summers and nuts for gathering in the fall.

Once she was gone, Melly informed me that the woman was called Aunt Pearl. She was the daughter of a former slave family who, after being freed, migrated to Muddy Ox to work in the saw mill and lumberyard. She could do the work of most men and even surpass some because of her strength and size. Melly said she had heard her grandpa tell someone that Aunt Pearl was well over six feet tall and probably weighed nearly three hundred pounds. I believed it!

Aunt Pearl approached Mr. Bertram, saying she was sent by Mr. Chaffin to be water person for a crew that would be arriving shortly. Mr. Chaffin occasionally, would send his crew to the Bertram's field when his crops were caught up. Aunt Pearl was directed to set the canteens down in the shade of the tree and told to wait on the other side of the field for the remainder of her crew.

I had seen a lot of black people, but never one who was from a former slave family, and I had never seen any person that size, of any nationality. It was sad to think that our backbreaking job in the cotton patch was even a step up from some of the jobs of her family's past.

We all made it through our Monday in the field, and six-o'clock finally came. Tara talked the entire way home. Mrs. Bertram didn't see the need to monitor Tara's conversation that time. It was all about school starting and her wanting me to meet her friends. I was going to love this school; she was sure of it! Also instead of her dad coming home that weekend, she, her mom and sisters were driving to St. Louis to go school shopping. In addition, they might go to the zoo Sunday morning before starting back home. Her adventure meant they wouldn't be in the field, come Friday. They needed that day for traveling so they could devote the entire Saturday for shopping. I selfishly thought how empty the field would seem without them. It wasn't fair for me to begrudge them the trip. The shopping trip would be fun and in addition, they'd get to see their dad. I hadn't seen my dad in over a month.

The wagon stopped, and I painfully got off. The hot sun had made for a hard day's work. I was drained and barely able to place one foot ahead of the other. My exhausted state quickly changed when Grandma met me at the edge of the yard with an announcement. Effie had given her a mattress. All we had to do was go carry it home. She already had a bed frame in our storage shed. With a little hard work and imagination, we could fix up the closed-in porch, adjacent to her bedroom, as a bedroom for me. I could have my own room! What great news! I forgot all about being tired as off we went to get my mattress.

On the way to Effie's I told Grandma about seeing Aunt Pearl in the field that day. She said she had seen her a few times around the Big Store, adding Aunt Pearl was hard to miss due to her size. Grandma confirmed that Aunt Pearl's parents were former slaves. She said she had a son who was rumored to have been fathered by her family's last owner. Her son's name was Dank Abraham, named for the slave owner, Daniel Abraham, as was customary. Aunt Pearl and Dank shared a shanty across the tracks.

Grandma shared a colorful story of how one day a group of men were sitting on the long church-type, benches that lined the front porch of the Big Store. As Aunt Pearl walked by, one of them jokingly proposed that if she could carry a two hundred pound stand of flour, to her shanty, a distance of about three-quarters of a mile, without putting it down, he would pay for it. A stand was a tightly sealed, one hundred or two hundred pound, metal or—in some cases—heavy corrugated cardboard barrel, used to store staples such as flour, beans, lard, or cornmeal for the winter.

Another man added sarcastically, "And if you can carry a watermelon at the same time, I'll pay for it too!"

Aunt Pearl never said a word but hoisted the two hundred pound stand of flour onto her shoulder, then—to their amazement—balanced the watermelon on her head and made for the other side of the tracks toward her shanty. Once there, she gave them a wave and disappeared inside. The store owner made the men pay for their bets and advised them to take notice of whom they were making bets with next time.

Grandma said she was told Aunt Pearl had a sister that was even taller and bigger than she was. Right now, either one of them would come in handy. My free mattress was so heavy that it felt like it had been stuffed with rocks!

Together we managed to manhandle the mattress home. We propped it up in what was going to be my room and had a plan to make it all work together, come the weekend. Having my own room like the McCrady girls had would be wonderful! Scarlett had a room of her own, being the oldest. Melly and Tara shared a room, but even if it had to be with each other, they didn't have to sleep in the same room with their mother or parents on the weekends their dad was home from St. Louis.

I was awakened the next morning by my bladder. For such occasions Grandma and I kept a night-bucket in our room, which allowed us to skip a middle-of-the night trip to our outside toilet. It also added the emptying of the night-bucket as one more chore to my list. I didn't mind. I would much more prefer the bucket-emptying trip to the toilet in daylight; besides, Grandma was afraid to go out in the dark at night. I would be taking that trip alone. Barely getting to the bucket in time, I soon realized I had slept long past my normal hour for getting up.

I was so exhausted from the previous hot day in the field in addition to wagging my mattress home, that I didn't hear the early morning rain storm. There would be no chopping today! The field was drenched. That meant a skimpy pay day, but it also meant we wouldn't have to wait until the weekend to work on my room. Grandma and I began as soon as we got breakfast and cleaning the kitchen behind us.

It didn't take us long to discover we had a double sized mattress for a twin sized bed. There was nothing to do but cut the mattress down to fit. It wasn't going to be an easy task, but we had no choice if I was to have a bed that had a mattress on it. We dragged it out on the front porch and placed it on a sheet for collecting the discarded padding, which was Grandma's idea for making the clean-up easier.

Having no measuring tape or stick, she used a string

of twine cut to the width of the bed frame and marked off how much of the mattress padding we would need to remove. Once that was decided, we slashed the covering and began digging out the extra cotton padding. Once we got it sized to fit the frame, Grandma took a big darning needle, threaded with a double strand of twine and reattached the covering. I held it tightly while she made precise loops. She then decided to stitch it once more for good measure, with the same looping action. We definitely wanted it to hold the first time. We never wanted to repeat that laborious procedure! It took the entire morning, but by noon it was ready to place on top of the coiled bedsprings.

The room was small; perhaps seven foot by ten foot of actual space after we allowed for a doorway and the makeshift closet that we had created when I first arrived. After all, it was first intended to be a porch, according to a self-proclaimed carpenter. All the workmanship had been crude with no finishing touches or details, but as in the case of my shoes, I didn't care. It was going to be my own private room. Grandma's and my plan for the day was to make that happen.

While on his daily run to the Post Office, Mr. Simpson was assigned to scan the big store for discarded cardboard boxes. His timely return provided us with enough boxes to cut down and use for insulation over the rough-cut boards that had been the walls, until then.

Mr. Simpson volunteered to do the cardboard insulation, allowing us to make a trip to the Big Store in search of a roll or two of wallpaper. This was a very nice gesture on Mr. Simpson's part. He could get it done in half the time that it would have taken Grandma and me. Mr. Simpson had a sweet side to him. People just didn't notice it much since he was always so quiet.

With lunch behind us, he started cutting down boxes, and we began our trek toward Muddy Ox and the Big Store. We could have probably found a better selection in the Dollar Store at Steele or Kennett, but neither of us wanted to wait. We also knew we had an opportunity to get our project completed without having to sacrifice a work day. Grandma gave the Good Lord the credit for that, as she quoted Psalms 37:4. It said if people would delight themselves in the things of the Lord, He'd give them the desires of their hearts. Well, God knew that it was the desire of both of our hearts for me to have a room of my own and a bed!

The Big Store actually had a better selection of wallpaper than either of us expected to find. I soon spied the very one I wanted. It was priced three rolls for a dollar. We got three rolls. Grandma bought a quarter's worth of big headed carpenter tacks. Tacking wall paper to the boards with such tacks was the only way she had ever seen it done before. It was also the only way to hang wallpaper on a wall without sheet rock. I didn't mind a few nail heads, I was just excited to be doing it at all. I chose a pattern of mauve and lavender starburst over a light grey background. I had a dollar and twenty nine cents left over from my earnings, and Grandma paid the balance from the money that Daddy had left for us.

There was one sliding window at the end of the room over my bed and a full-size window on the outside wall. We found a pair of plastic curtains the exact shade of the lavender in the wallpaper. A bedspread would have to wait for me to make some more money, and for another trip to Steele or Kennett.

Mr. Simpson was putting up the last sheet of cardboard as we arrived. We had my tiny room papered in no time at all. Grandma measured, I cut it, and Mr. Simpson did the tacking.

We didn't have curtain rods, but a triple strand of twine stretched very tightly across the top of each window worked nicely. After cutting one of the curtains to fit the small sliding window over the bed, I had a matching piece of plastic left to cover a wooden box which became an instant vanity table for my hairbrush, comb and hand mirror.

My room was complete and I could sleep in it that very night! Mr. Simpson suggested he re-string the wire we hung for the closet. He was able to stretch it tighter so it didn't sag in the middle. Grandma and I re-stacked her jars of canned goods and extra bedding to leave even more space for my clothes. We decided it might be needed, now that I was a working girl and would be increasing my wardrobe considerably. I couldn't wait for the girls to return to tell them about my new room.

Since I wouldn't need it any more, Grandma could now use the second bed in her room for company, should we get any. She didn't say, but I knew she expected Daddy to return eventually. Miss Katty and

Sadie showed up just as we finished and were very impressed with our handiwork.

"Mrs. Strom, y'all have been at it all day. Why don't you and Meryl Jean come and eat with us tonight?" Miss Katty invited.

I truly hoped Grandma would accept her offer for three good reasons. First of all, there wasn't a lot in our refrigerator suitable for gleaning that night. Second, we were hungry. Third, Grandma had her special dishes, but Miss Katty indisputably made the best pot of white beans in the whole country. There would be no need to ask her what we would be having for dinner. That lady made a pot of her beans every day of her life. With that much practice, there was no wonder she could make them so tasty.

If we were lucky, she had made one of her skillet cakes too. I never knew for sure how she did it, but her skillet cakes were just special. She threw all the ingredients together without even a recipe. It was her icing, however, that made them so wonderful. She mixed up a little cocoa, butter, sugar, vanilla flavoring, milk, and corn starch. Then she said she held her mouth just right to make the icing. It was poured over the cake, still hot from the oven. By serving time the crusty, glazed icing, tasted like a cross between fudge candy and cake icing. I was not convinced about the holding of her mouth part, but she evidently did something special. I hadn't ever tasted a cake like it before, nor have I until this day.

The McCrady girls said when they were younger, anytime they played with Sadie, they wished Miss Katty would make one of her cakes and invite them to have a piece.

I held my breath until Grandma told her we'd come. This was definitely a blessed day. As soon as we stepped into her kitchen, the first thing I saw on her counter was one of Miss Katty's cakes!

Chapter Ten

Mr. Simpson's Short-lived Control

THE FIELD WE were to pick the next day had been recently plowed. The sun-dried and hardened gumbo clods felt like sharp clumps of concrete beneath my thin-soled shoes. The conditions would be better after another plowing, but that day was going to be a very difficult walking day for me.

Mrs. Bertram called for dinner. The field cleared immediately, with the black folk going in one direction and the Mexicans in another. I sought the shade of the Bertram's wagon to eat my dinner and to get off my feet for a while.

I most surely was going to try out some of Grandma's smelly bag balm after supper that evening. Would I wear my boy shoes to the field if I still had them? The mere thought of it caused me to cringe. Surely there was another way. The McCrady girls didn't wear boy shoes to work in. Of course, their shoes cost them much more than a dollar a pair and had thicker soles. I had no other choice. My feet would just have to toughen up like the rest of me. I was not ever going to wear boy shoes again.

That evening, Grandma questioned my limp as soon as she noticed it and had an immediate solution, which she promised we'd get to after supper. I rushed through my sponge bath and joined her on the swing. It didn't take long to figure out she had done that fix before. Using the leftover cardboard from the boxes we used to insulate my room—of course, she never threw them away—she precisely cut an insert for each of my shoes. I feared there wouldn't be enough room inside the shoes for the cardboard cushion and my feet too. Not to worry, my wide feet had already stretched the shoes out enough for that. It didn't matter. I'd get ten more pairs of dollar shoes if I had to.

The make-shift inserts worked wonderfully. I had no problem negotiating the gumbo clods the rest of the week.

It was now Friday, but working in the fields wasn't the same without the girls. The silence made for a very long day. I started chopping to the rhythm of the black spirituals that drifted across the field and tried to think about our Saturday trip to town the next afternoon.

That night at supper Grandma told me that Mr. Simpson would not be working at all on our usual Saturday half day. Miss Katty had to see a doctor in Kennett concerning some health issues and the doctor would be in his office only until noon. They figured starting earlier, and getting there while almost everyone else was still in the field, would give them a better chance of getting in to see him. I hated to give up the money but was glad once again to skip the half day of work. I'd still have money enough for a couple more pairs of cheap canvas shoes. With a little luck I could also find a lavender bedspread somewhere in town.

Grandma had yet another surprise for me as I arrived home from the field that evening. She had found a full length mirror for the wall behind the boxed vanity table in my room. One corner was broken at the bottom, but we decided that I could hang it low enough to cover up the broken part.

"A lot of people won't keep a broken mirror because of superstitions and the fear of it bringing them bad luck. I found it tossed into a trash pile behind the corner store. Christians shouldn't be superstitious," she stated, then continued. "I'm not in the least. It'll be perfect for your room."

After we cleaned it up and hid the damaged corner behind the box, no one was ever the wiser. I didn't know if they were superstitious or not; so I hadn't planned to tell Melly and her sisters that the mirror was broken. They would be home Monday, and I was looking forward to showing them my room since they didn't have time to come and see it before they left for St. Louis. That was all right; it gave me a little more time to find the perfect bedspread. I knew my room wasn't as nice as theirs, but it was beautiful to me.

Grandma and I went to bed even earlier than usual to be ready for when Simp and Miss Katty wanted to leave for town. Since the doctor Miss Katty was seeing had his practice in Kennett, Sadie didn't get to choose the town that Saturday. I actually preferred shopping in Kennett anyway.

Sadie was not her usual whining self that trip. Could it be she was finally going to act her age? Grandma and I were dropped off on the square, allowing the Simpsons time to get to the doctor's office shortly after it opened. We offered to let Sadie come with us, but she would have none of that. She never got very far from her mother.

As soon as they turned the corner, Grandma shared, "I hope they don't get bad news about Katty."

For the first time, it dawned on me that Miss Katty was not made of cast iron and could have something seriously wrong with her.

"What do they think it might be?"

"They're not sure. It seems that nothing she eats, sets well with her. She has become very weak lately from not being able to keep anything down. I've noticed her losing weight and asked her about it, but she didn't give me any real answer as to why."

Then, I realized why Sadie was so quiet. Simp was even less talkative than usual, which meant he said nothing. They were scared to death about the doctor's visit. Also Miss Katty's name and the word weak had never been found in the same sentence as far as I had ever heard.

"Grandma, I didn't realize she'd been sick," I mumbled. Now, I was also frightened for her.

"Well, Katty is loud and big as life most of the time, but she can also be a very private person if it's about her. We'll have to pray and trust that God will take care of her in this. I have seen her overcome malaria, deliver still-born twins, and about die giving birth to Sadie, but I've never seen Katty in this shape before." There was no doubt that Grandma was truly worried about her dear friend.

We were at the door of the Dollar Store when we saw the trio who just dropped us off, coming down the street toward us.

"That sure didn't take very long, what did you find out?" Grandma inquired.

"Nothin' we didn't find out not one thing," Mr. Simpson spouted.

Grandma was about to comment when Miss Katty added "Mrs. Strom, there is no way we can go see that doctor. Why, he wants fifteen dollars just to look at me. Why that's almost half a week's wages. And, that was just to start, no telling how much it would cost us in the long run."

"I told her we'd make it somehow. She needs to go on in and see him," a worried Mr. Simpson argued.

"It's nothing new. I've been having spells with my stomach now for over a year. It'll be okay, I'll be careful about what I eat. It'll be okay," Miss Katty interrupted.

"Well, we'll see. It seems to me to be gettin' worse. I'll be doing somethin' to get you to the doctor. You wait and see," promised a desperate Mr. Simpson.

Sadie had been unnaturally patient during all that

exchange, but now she was in town and wanted to make the most of it. The concern over her mother was short-lived. I guessed she thought all was fine, since Miss Katty didn't see the doctor after all.

"Momma, let's go to the five and dime store. I want to go to the store now," Sadie demanded.

"Okay, we're going," Miss Katty conceded.

Mr. Simpson gave her a look, but he was over-ruled. "Simp, I am not hurting right now. It might even go away altogether. We're here, so let's not waste the time or the gasoline for coming. It'll be okay. There is no need to disappoint Sadie. Mrs. Strom and Meryl have some things to get too. It'll be okay." She had now reassured him again that it would be okay, entirely too many times and still wasn't truly convincing.

He reluctantly gave in, but he wasn't happy about it. They went down the street to the five and dime. He accompanied them that time, probably to keep a watchful eye on his headstrong wife.

Grandma and I darted into the Dollar Store. I had to admit; I also put Miss Katty's sickness aside, in hopes of finding a lavender bedspread. This had to be my lucky day. The perfect spread was hidden underneath several others, as though it had been hiding and waiting just for me. It was even marked down to three dollars and fifty cents due to a small rip on one corner which Grandma could easily repair in no time. Besides, it was on the side of the bed that was up against the wall. It would drape behind the bed and be out of sight. No one other than Grandma and me would ever have to know that it had been ripped. It was just the finishing touch that my bedroom needed.

Monday morning as the tractor halted, and I got on the cotton wagon, it was my turn to be the chatter box. I couldn't stop talking about my room. I also did a little rubbing in about our supper invite to Miss Katty's and the cake. I asked the girls over after our work day to see my room first hand. They too, were excited for me to have my own room.

We chose our rows and got started. Mrs. Bertram cautioned us that if we were going to continue talking we needed to be sure and keep working too, while we did it.

That evening, when the girls came over, they were impressed just as I thought they'd be. We sat for a long time on my bed, talking about the coming school year. I confided in them my concerns of being a new kid in school. Then we talked about my biggest fear, which was that I might be made fun of as I was in my other schools. They scoffed it off as if it was all in my head. They said they had never thought of me as being fat. Scarlett stepped back to look at me as though she was seeing me for the first time ever. She again assured me she thought there would not be a problem at all.

That was easy for them to say. Not one of them had an ounce of fat on her anywhere. They could walk into any shoe store and choose the shoe of their dreams. They grew up with the kids at that school. Of course they wouldn't think there would be a problem. I had shell-shock. One of Grandma's favorite sayings was, *"a burnt child fears the fire.*" I had been in and out of the fire of ridicule for as long as I could remember. I sure hoped they were right. It didn't matter; I was there to stay.

MR. SIMPSON WAS noticeably absent in the field the next day. Grandma would probably know why he wasn't there. I'd find out when I got home. I hoped that Miss Katty didn't have another one of her stomach attacks or something.

I had finally gotten to where I could keep up my row without help from Mrs. Bertram. She wasn't big on compliments, but I knew she was pleased with me because she gave me a half-smile as she passed by me that morning.

I also had become an expert on the difference between morning glories and cotton. However, since the cotton plants had grown considerably, it really wasn't that much of a problem any longer. Cotton and morning glories don't look alike at all after they get a certain height.

That night Grandma and I were finishing our supper when Mr. Simpson pecked on the screen door. His visits were not as common as Miss Katty and Sadie's, especially not solo visits. He obviously had something on his mind.

"Y'all 'bout done with supper?" he asked.

Grandma invited him to pull up a chair and offered him some peach cobbler. He nodded in acceptance as he sat down.

"Just wanted to tell you I took a job with the railroad today. I won't be helping Mr. Bertram in the field any more. As soon as my insurance gets started, I want Kat to go back to that doctor. She doesn't say much about it, but those stomach attacks of hers are coming around more often. The last few spells have been pretty fierce. She won't go see the doctor and run up a bill. Taking this job is the only way I can get insurance for her. I'm gettin' pretty worried 'bout her."

"I was wondering why you weren't there today." I was glad to let him know that he'd been missed.

"That's good, Simp. I am glad you got a job like that instead of working your life away and breaking your back in the cotton field," Grandma said while she served up his cobbler and coffee.

"Well, Mrs. Strom, you know the Bible says it's a dishonorable thing when a man can't take care of his family. I can't tell you where it can be found, but I know it's in there. We've always had food and what we needed to get by, but this thing with Kat is something that we can't turn our backs on. She has tried every kind of home remedy you can think of, but nothing has helped. I can't just keep doin' what I been doin' and let her die from something that maybe could be fixed with insurance.

Railroad work is not easy. It's just a different kind of hard than the cotton field. I've never done any kinda' work like that before, but I know I can learn like the rest of 'em." It sounded as though he was wanting to reassure himself as much as he wanted to tell us about his new job.

"Simp, you'll do good, I know you will. I'm proud of you. I am glad to hear you care and know what the Bible teaches." Grandma felt better now about maybe how they might see going to church a little more needful.

"I know what to do. I just don't always do it. I'm gonna' try to do better from now on, and I'm gonna' start by takin' this job and takin' care of my wife," he said proudly.

To others, it might have sounded as though Mr. Simpson was trying to apologize for taking a job other than field work. Instead, we knew he was confirming out loud that he had done the right thing. Miss Katty had always made it plain that she didn't want him working outside the cotton field. She was like that. She was not open to much self-improvement. She saw the field as something safe and familiar. Working on a public job was just that—public. The less they rubbed elbows with the public, the better she felt.

She never saw an education as particularly im-portant. She'd already said that she would be okay with it if Sadie just went as far as the sixth grade in school. That was three grades more than either she or Simp had attended. She liked for things to stay the same and remain simple. She felt more in control that way. What her husband was saying, without actually saying it, was that he knew he had a battle on his hands but by telling Grandma, he hoped maybe she could talk to his wife and get her to listen and understand.

GRANDMA WAS ABLE to win Miss Katty over to Mr. Simpson's way of thinking about the railroad job and its being their only answer to her health problems. She admitted to Grandma that she also knew her problem was getting worse thus confirming that Simp had made the right choice.

As soon as his insurance became effective, Katty agreed to go to the doctor again. That turn of events didn't happen any time too soon. The doctor sent her to a specialist in Memphis as soon as he could get her there.

Grandma offered to help out with Sadie during Miss Katty's hospital stay. Katty surprisingly agreed to her offer, letting us know even more how her condition must have worsened. Sadie was to stay with Grandma during the day, and she and Simp went home right after supper each night. Grandma insisted they have supper with us until Miss Katty's recovery and Simp agreed.

That was when I noticed a big change in Sadie. It was the first time in her almost ten years that she had been more than a leash away from her mother. She was a different, less demanding child in her mother's absence. She and I sort of bonded in a sense. Sadie communicated quite well without her mother there to finish her sentences. This confirmed Miss Katty's overpowering need to keep her young child in babyish ways and not let her grow up and mature. Sadie was more likeable and pleasant when her enabler was not around.

A healthier Katty returned three weeks later, feeling much better, with a little sack of gall stones to keep as a reminder of her problem and what could have been her certain death. That was the end of her stomach problems.

However, as soon as she could, she returned to her enabling ways with Sadie and convinced Mr. Simpson to quit his railroad job and go back to the cotton field. Once that happened, things were back to normal for her, and she felt in control of her simple little world again.

Chapter Eleven

A New Home, A New School, A New Name

THE FIRST DAY of school was quickly approaching. I had ten pairs each of canvas shoes, underwear and bobby socks, along with several new outfits. A pair of brown girl shoes with a purse to match shared space in my closet alongside the first pair of girl shoes I had purchased. Both pairs would have to be saved for church and special occasions. Either pair would be painfully brutal if I tried to wear them to school every day, not to mention, they would have been short-lived. Canvas shoes and bobby socks were fine for school. They were what most of the girls wore anyway.

Ten pairs of canvas shoes could have been seen as an extravagance to some, but not to me. I needed that many pairs if I planned to wear them every day. Not much workmanship went into shoes costing only one dollar a pair. My wide feet could stretch out a pair of those cheap shoes, causing them to burst at the seams in less than six weeks. I didn't care; I would buy twice as many pairs rather than wear boy shoes again. Grandma and I were determined for me to have enough money saved for my book fees. She constantly reinforced that *"people must learn to plan ahead in cotton country."*

The school terms in that part of the country were governed by the cotton seasons. The first split-term began when chopping season was over and lasted until picking time.

As soon as the fields were white with cotton, classes were halted, thus allowing the students to help their families with the harvest and providing income for purchase of winter provisions as well as fall and winter school clothes. The second split-term session began immediately after the majority of the cotton crop had been picked.

The McCrady girls promised me that more money could be made picking cotton than chopping it. They also warned it would be much harder work.

Remembering my blister, I couldn't imagine how it could possibly have been any worse than my chopping cotton experience had been. I wasn't going to worry about that right then. The first split-term session was about to start, and I was ready.

Muddy Ox School was smaller than the school in Illinois or any other school I had ever attended. Everyone knew everybody's name down to the elementary students. It would have been safe to say, everyone even knew everybody's dog's name in the town too.

The girls continued to assure me I would *just love* the

school. Of course, it was the only school either of them had ever attended. What did they have to compare it with? I had gone to many schools and was teased unmercifully in every one of them. Their worst nightmare held no comparison to what I had been through.

That was then and this was now. I was adamant that if I never allowed the first person to start with the taunting, then no one else would follow. I wouldn't have it!

Tara was her usual bubbly self as we hurried down the hall toward my new homeroom teacher, Mr. Ness. She was thrilled to be the one to introduce her transplanted friend from St. Louis. I hadn't actually lived in St. Louis, but few people had heard of Brookstown, Illinois. Everyone had heard of St. Louis. Brookstown was a mere few miles across the Mississippi River and a jaunt down the road from St. Louis. It was close enough to be referred to as St. Louis if it got more attention.

I was Tara's friend and she knew me first. My Grandmother was her neighbor, and I lived with her now because my mother had died. Kids without mothers and being raised by grandparents, wasn't common in those days. How special could that get?

Mr. Carlton began as he was reading my transcript. "Now, let's see, you moved here from Illinois. Actually, it looks as though you have moved quite often. Your grandmother is Mrs. Strom and your name is…"

"Jean, her name is Jean and we have been friends for a long time." Tara chimed in. "My grandma taught her how to chop cotton. Her mother died, and now she lives with her grandma, Mrs. Strom. We are neighbors," Tara recounted just in case he didn't get it the first time.

"Jean, hmmm, it says here your name is Meryl. You want to be called Meryl or Jean?" He asked still never looking up from the form as he awaited my answer.

"Her name is Meryl Jean, but we all call her Jean." Tara couldn't help but interrupt again.

Mr. Ness finally made eye contact with me to see if I agreed with Tara as to what my name really was. I hesitated for a moment, *"Meryl the barrel."* That was what I was called at the other school. Then, I thought *Jean...nothing rhymed with Jean but lean.*

"Jean, call me Jean," I said with surety. I'd have a new home, new school and a new name. Meryl the barrel would be history.

"Well, Jean, we're glad to have you here at Muddy Ox High School. I'll be your homeroom teacher. Your first hour class each morning will be in this room. I'm sure Tara will be glad to show you where the library is so you can pick up your textbooks. Here are your assignments and schedule. See you tomorrow." Mr. Ness smiled, shaking his head as he handed me my lists of assignments and required book list.

Tara chattered non-stop, telling me where everything was and all about the school, as we made our way down the hall and into the library. Once we were inside, Mrs. Pendergrass, the librarian, looked at Tara and pointed to the *quiet* sign.

Tara made the introduction in a whisper, said she

would meet me for dinner, then rushed off to her first class. Hearing that she planned for us to meet for dinner took me by surprise. I hadn't thought of that.

Dinner might happen for her, but it wasn't going to happen for me. I couldn't eat in an open setting. Everyone would be watching the new fat girl eat. Besides, I wouldn't have money for a dinner every day, even if I wanted to have one. I'd need to quickly come up with an excuse that Tara would accept. My new classmates couldn't find out that the new girl from St. Louis didn't have money to buy dinner!

The morning went well. I had yet to hear one offensive word from anyone. This was a good day. The dinner bell rang, and Tara came bouncing down the hall with several friends trailing behind. It was obvious they were coming to meet me for us to go to dinner. I had to think fast.

"Hey, Jean, are you ready to go?" Her voice echoed in the hall as Tara approached.

"I'm sorry; I just remembered that my dad is supposed to come by the school today at noon. Can we do it another day?" The words spilled out of my mouth as though they had been the God's honest truth.

"But Betty Ann, Carla, Patty and Mattie Lynn all want to meet you." Tara's disappointment was evident.

"Hi, I'm Jean Strom. Tara has told me a lot about you all." I introduced myself as to not appear unsociable. "I'm really anxious to meet you too, but I just can't go to dinner with you all today. My dad is supposed to come by the school and sign some papers. I need to meet him at the office when he gets here. You think we can do this another time?"

I lied twice, once to Tara and now to her friends. I haven't heard from my dad since he left those ruts in Grandma's yard.

Somehow, it was enough to satisfy them for the moment. It sounded like something that was supposed to happen on the first day of school. They seemed to buy it as they swished off toward the school cafeteria. I headed toward the office and didn't look back until I thought they were completely out of sight.

I felt awful, as though I surely had this big cloud hovering over my head, drenching me with guilt. Lying was something my mother was very stern about. She would have been so ashamed of me. I hadn't planned to lie. Those were just the first words out of my mouth.

A similar thing had happened when I was in the third grade in Brookstown Elementary School. I was playing tag during noon hour recess with several other children. It was an unseasonably cool day, and my mother had insisted that I wear a coat. Before long, I had become heated from running, and the coat was soon tossed aside. One of my playmates while reaching to tag me out, accidentally ripped the sleeve of my dress. The bell rang and recess was over. The others ran through the wide open double doors, leaving me lingering and scared. My coat would cover the rip for a while, but what was I to do once I had to take it off? I was sure some one would say it ripped because I was fat. It never took much for the teasing to get started.

The second bell rang just as I made it into the room. I quietly slid into my desk with my coat still in place. I thought I might have gotten by with it, until Richard Black, a boy who took great pleasure in humiliating me, discovered that I was still wearing my coat.

"Why are you still wearing your coat, Meryl the Barrel? Don't all that fat keep you warm enough?"

Insults spewed from his twisted mouth like poison darts being hurled toward a defenseless target.

"Mr. Bogden needs me in the office. I have a test to make up from when I was absent. They're coming to get me soon," I whispered. Had the cruel child looked closely enough, he would have seen my face pale with fear. The excuse had satisfied him for the moment; so he turned around and left me alone. What was I going to do? How much longer would it be before he noticed that no one was coming for me and there was no test?

I flinched as a pencil dropped on the floor behind me. Somehow, I had held back the tears. I was a mess! My palms were sweating, and I was sick to my stomach from the fear that the others would, before long, also notice that I was still wearing my coat.

"Mrs. Cudow," summoned a soft, sweet voice.

"Yes," my teacher replied as she addressed the person standing at classroom door.

"I've come for Meryl Strom. She is needed in the office for a make-up test." The secretary stood waiting for my teacher's response. I knew she was the secretary from the office, but to me she was an angel. An Angel that was rescuing a nine year old child from absolute doom!

"That is fine. Meryl, you may leave. Be sure and take your books and assignments for tomorrow and don't forget your…"

The test would take the remainder of the day. I wouldn't be expected back to class. Mrs. Cudow had been about to remind me to get my coat, before she saw that I was already wearing it. Puzzled, but immediately approached by another student, she let it go and motioned for me to leave.

I gathered my things and gave my oppressor, Richard Wells, a know-all stare as I left the classroom.

Then I followed my angel, the secretary, to the office. I finished the test just as the last bell rang. I was more than ready to get home to my mother's comforting embrace.

That had been four years ago, but my heart was again racing and my palms were sweating merely from the memory. I couldn't believe I had just done it again.

The girls would never know if Daddy came or not. Tara probably wouldn't remember to ask. I would know. I would know that I had lied. If by chance Tara did remember, I could maybe tell her that he never showed up. That would be the truth. Anyone familiar with my dad knew that he was not likely to do much of anything he was expected to do.

As I walked past the office, the receptionist came to the door and asked, "Are you Jean…hmm Mer… Jean…Strom?"

"Yes," I said, as I disregarded her confusion.

"You have a message," she said as she offered me a note.

I couldn't believe my eyes! It was from my dad. He had found my birth certificate and shot records crumpled under the front seat of the car. I figured he found them while he was reaching for his pint of whiskey. He said he planned to be back to Grandma's this weekend and would bring them so I could have them for school. I was supposed to have had those documents that day, but since he called, the school said they would give me until the next week to bring them in.

I did have a guardian angel. I was sure of it now. This would cancel my lie altogether. I could truthfully say that my dad couldn't make it but he called the school.

I was in shock because of the phone call but also surprised at Daddy taking care of an important matter. Maybe he was going to change. I guessed I could judge that better after seeing him on the weekend. I had to admit I'd missed him and I was excited that he would be coming home. No doubt Grandma would be happy to see him and be proud he called the school. He hadn't mentioned it in the note, but my birthday was going to be in a week. Maybe he remembered and was going to surprise me with something. Maybe that was another reason for him coming home.

I went from feeling happiness about Daddy's coming home to feeling a wave of sadness in remembering how my orderly mother would have never sent me to a new school without all of my important papers. I couldn't look back or let the sadness linger. That was Meryl. I was Jean now. I could get my own papers to school...as soon as I got them from Daddy.

Chapter Twelve

Meryl Finds A New Friend

TARA AND I were in the same sixth hour class. As soon as the bell rang, we rushed to our lockers, met at the front doors, and walked home together. She was rambling about all of the activities and clubs she intended to join. She wanted to be on the yearbook committee. She planned to try out for cheerleading. If she made cheerleader, she'd be going to all of the games. She was confident her grade point average would get her invited to Beta Club and on and on.

As we walked along, I realized that most of her intended activities were way beyond me. First of all, we had no car, no phone, and hardly any money. It was plain to see I was not cheerleading material. I hadn't made the greatest grades in Illinois; so I wasn't sure of Beta Club. My grades suffered a lot from all of the absences due to Daddy's impulsive trips.

Grandma would never hear of me being gone at night for anything, especially ball games. Not only was she protective, she was afraid of staying nights alone. Grandma wanted me to finish high school and do well, but she didn't see a need for all of the extra curricular activities. She also saw Rock N Roll, dancing, and the current fashions as devilish and was not open to them in the least. It might have been the Rock N Roll explosion of the Fifties and Sixties to the rest of the world, but I was living under a rock. It passed right over me.

It was obvious that Tara and I would not be on the same social levels at all. We would still love one another, work together in the fields, maybe even get together in the evenings if her calendar allowed, but no way was I going to be the social butterfly that she was going to be. I would need to find my own circle of school friends other than the McCrady girls.

We arrived at Tara's house first. Her mother was waiting beyond the screen door, as we arrived. Walking away, I could hear Tara happily sharing the events of the day with her mother. Hardly anyone had air conditioners during that time. Casual conversations could easily be heard through the open screened doors and windows. Tara was so excited, I heard most of hers halfway home.

With no mid-day meal, I was hungry. Grandma was sitting in the swing, and no doubt, supper was not far from being ready. She felt bad about me not eating all day, but I assured her it wasn't a problem. I told her I didn't mind not having money for dinner at school, I wanted to try and drop a few pounds anyway.

She was also pleasantly surprised to hear that Daddy called the school and planned to be home that weekend. She was probably already mentally planning a feast for her prodigal son, upon his arrival, as we spoke.

I told her about Mr. Ness and my new name while we ate. She was still going to call me Meryl, but if everyone else wanted to call me Jean, it was all right with her. After we cleaned the kitchen, she went over to talk with Effie Walby. I tackled my homework assignments and was finishing the last math problem as she returned.

Effie sent us a couple of homemade cinnamon buns to enjoy later as we relaxed out on the porch swing. The stars were even brighter than usual. The moonlight fell across the rocks in the lane as tree frogs treated us to an evening concert. It was peaceful out on Grandma's back porch. I loved it there.

Bedtime came early on school nights, and to be honest, I was ready. I dabbed my dampened toothbrush into the small mound of baking soda in the palm of my hand and began brushing my teeth before bed. I had to get used to the taste of baking soda; there was no extra money for things like toothpaste.

I thought of how much I looked forward to school the next day. What a difference from the way I'd felt at my schools in Illinois, where I dreaded to walk through the front doors of the building each morning.

I realized—right before I drifted off to sleep—that I did my school assignments on my own, with no prompting from anyone. I did them because I wanted to, and it felt right.

Choosing what to wear the next morning took me longer than usual. I'd never had so many clothes before.

I had noticed that most of the girls at school wore a touch of make-up. I'd never worn make-up, but I was sure going to get some, come cotton picking time—if I could talk Grandma into it. She thought makeup was another of those worldly things and frowned upon it.

Trying to fit in had caused me to be quite critical of myself. I thought my eye brows were too light and sparse and my lips were too thin. I wasn't going to need blush, or rouge as Grandma would call it; my cheeks were rosy enough. Actually, I saw them as too rosy. Perhaps a little pressed powder would tone them down a bit. I'd have to wait until the time was right to convince her that I needed to wear make-up to fit in with the other girls.

Mr. Ness was pleased and impressed as I laid my homework on his desk. I saw nothing but friendly faces as I moved from class to class. That was the way school should have been. That was the way life should have been.

Tara had cheerleading tryouts during the noon hour; so I didn't have to make any excuses to her concerning dinner that day. I pretended to organize my locker until everyone cleared the halls then darted out the south door of the building. The noon sun was blinding, but it felt good.

A new girl who had been in Mr. Ness's class that morning was sitting on the grass, leaned against the wall, and reading a book.

"Hello," I said.

She shaded her eyes from the sun with her hand while trying to look up to see me.

"Mind if I sit with you? You're new too; aren't you?" I asked.

She timidly made me welcome. "My name is— Jean—Jean Strom," I said, almost forgetting my new name.

"Hi, I'm Polly Evans. Yes, this is my first day," she said as she welcomed me to sit next to her.

"Did you already have dinner?" I inquired, trying to make small talk.

"No...I wasn't hungry," she replied.

Not very far into our conversation, it was evident that she didn't have cafeteria money either. Her dad was a sharecropper. They had an enormous family. She was the second oldest of seven children. The two youngest weren't even school age yet. They had recently moved to Muddy Ox from Caraway, Arkansas. Her dad followed the crops from season to season, picking strawberries in Arkansas, grapes in Michigan, peaches in Illinois, and now the cotton harvest, in Muddy Ox.

Polly hoped her dad would decide to stay put at least until she could finish high school. She was tired of starting new schools. I think, if it was possible, she had been to more schools than I had.

When it was my turn to swap stories, I told her about my mother dying and my coming to live with Grandma. I skirted around certain facts about my dad. I told her he was away working and added that he was coming home that weekend. I left out the part about him being hot tempered and having a drinking problem.

She found my only child status fascinating. Always having so many siblings in her household, she couldn't begin to imagine being an only child. Catching me off-guard, she bluntly asked why I wasn't eating dinner.

Before I knew it, I confessed about also not having cafeteria money. Then I shared a little of how I was trying to avoid any unwanted remarks about my weight. Her reaction was like Scarlett's. She too, didn't know why I was so self-conscious, saying she didn't think I was extremely overweight, compared to others she had seen.

True, I was not grossly overweight, and I carried what weight I had, very well. I also carried emotional scars that made me uncomfortable and kept me on guard most of the time. My weight might not have been gross, but I was big enough to get teased. I had to stick to my plan and not let the first person get by with cutting words so that others would follow.

The bell rang. We were so busy sharing about each other and making friends that we didn't notice the noon hour had flown by. It was obvious that she was not going to be a social butterfly either. If anything, she had less than I had. Grandma was going to let me keep what money I made from working in the fields. This poor girl's wages got added to providing for their large family. When the crops were gone for the season, so was their income. Suddenly I felt almost wealthy. I was actually rich, compared to poor Polly.

Chapter Thirteen

Daddy's Home

THE REST OF the school week went by uneventfully. When Tara saw that I was spending so much time with Polly, she stopped trying to work me into her group. I liked her friends and they liked me, but I was trying to avoid the embarrassment of declining invitations, when I knew my lack of funds and Grandma's short rope would make accepting nearly impossible. Polly also wasn't going to fit in the group for many of the same reasons.

The one place that Tara, her circle of friends, Polly, and I could be considered as equals was Chorus Class. Polly had a nice voice also; this was another thing we had in common. Neither she nor I had any inhibitions in Chorus Class.

Polly was a bus rider, so we said our goodbyes as soon as class was over. It was Friday and we wouldn't see each other again until Monday. Tara made cheerleader, of course, and was staying after school for practice. With a mind full of aimless thoughts, I made my way down the black-top road toward home, with only my shadow as a companion.

The high grass by the road ditch was being switched and swirled by the warm afternoon winds. It reminded me of the raindrops that had pooled along the car window's edge when we had made our move to Grandma's, also of the *day of the whirlwind* in the cotton patch. The road ditch was brimming with water, as a result of recent rains. I heard the buzzing of dragon flies and was entertained by their methodical dance as they swooped along the ditch water, in search of food. I kept a watchful eye for an occasional snake that was known to slither out of the water to sun on the river rock along side the road. I couldn't see them, but I knew there was an abundance of crawdads burrowed into the muddy bottom of the ditch.

Thinking of the crawdads brought a memory of my first and last experience with the little critters. I must have been around eight years old. During one of our visits to Grandma's, several years before Mama died, we had no sooner pulled onto Grandma's gravel lane, when I saw the McCrady girls, all three of them, wading in the road ditch along side the lane. Recognizing our car, they started waving and yelling for me to come join them. Sid Carson had offered to pay them a penny for each ordinary crawdad they brought him, plus three cents for each red one they could find. Crawdads were excellent fishing bait. Catfish especially couldn't resist the red ones. They were squealing with joy saying, "Jean, come help us, we found a baby lobster," referring to a red crawdad they had just dug out of the mud.

I gave Grandma, a quick hug before scurrying over to where they were standing knee-deep in the over-flowing road ditch. I agreed to hold the bucket and help them keep count, but Sid Carson couldn't have paid me enough money to pick up one of the little scrunched-faced, beady-eyed things. Why, they had pinchers! No, the girls could have kept every penny that they made as far as I was concerned. I was confident that before we all made our trip to the corner store, I would have been able to scrounge a nickel or two out of Mama. Just the smell of the stinky things squirming around in the bait bucket was enough for me. The McCrady sisters and I had shared so many happy, adolescent memories, long before I had actually become their neighbor and school chum.

Hearing the whirring engine of an approaching car, I moved far to the side of the road. I was startled to be met with the unmistakable eyes of Nate McDougal, as the long, black sedan with a star encircled by the word Sheriff, sailed by. Those had been the same cold, steel-gray eyes that had peered past Grandma, the evening that he claimed to be looking for his dog and, once again, made me shiver with fear.

Knowing that the authorities obviously had him in custody, where he wouldn't be able to harm anyone, had given me a slight sense of calm. I was anxious to get home to tell Grandma what I'd seen, so she could be at peace about him also.

The porch swing was vacant, but the aroma of fried chicken coming from her kitchen left no doubt about where she could be found. I purposely didn't look toward the chicken pen. I was bothered that the same chickens that we had seen hatched from eggs, pecking and scratching in the pen daily, could occasionally wind up on our supper plates. Grandma had said I'd have to get past that, now that we raised our own food of sorts.

The wonderful taste of fresh fried chicken could over shadow any guilt of how it got there, if I would just not think about it while at the supper table.

Grandma must have gotten Miss Katty to wring its neck. She had a weak wrist from an improperly treated broken bone in years past and didn't have the strength to do the deed herself. She had busily prepared a feast fit for a king. My dad hadn't arrived yet, but she was positive he was on his way.

While setting the table for three, I proceeded to tell her about Nate in the police car. She, too, was relieved to have him out of the way for a while. Of course, Nate was far down on her list of priorities at the moment; there were biscuits to take out of the oven.

We finally ate and cleared the table, after we had waited as long as we could. With still no sign of Daddy, Grandma was obviously disappointed and so was I. We sat on the porch swing later than usual but decided there wasn't anything to do but to go on to bed.

"Maybe he had to work and got a late start. He'll probably be here in the morning for breakfast." She gave him the benefit of every doubt imaginable, short of conceding it was possible he wouldn't show up at all.

Once in bed, I rolled over, tucked the sheets in

around me and made my *sleep nest*. I heard Grandma beyond the thin wall that separated our bedrooms, as she whispered her night prayers. She never neglected the nightly ritual of saying her prayers before bed. My dad always topped her list, with that night being no exception. After I heard her crawl into bed, all was quiet except for the night noises. We slept with the windows raised, and there was never a shortage of night noises. I could hear the chirping crickets, the leaves blowing in the trees, the distant barking of a neighbor's dog or Miss Katty's tomcats howling and hissing and getting into fights. Thank heavens for screens on the windows. The hum of the mosquitoes let me know they were there and ready to bite.

We hadn't more than drifted off to sleep before we heard a banging coming from the kitchen. Bolting out of bed and peeking around the door facing for a full view, we saw that it was Daddy. Grandma flicked on the lights as she rushed to let him in. I trailed closely behind.

"Hello Son. Thank the Lord you're all right. I was worried about you. Did you have trouble? Did you have to work late?" The door swung open and he staggered in. I detected a strong smell of whiskey as I hugged and greeted him with a kiss.

If Grandma had noticed the whiskey smell, she never let it be known. "Are you hungry, Son?" She tried as usual to make wrongs right with food.

He stumbled to the table as she placed all the leftovers before him. She started to warm them up, before he told her that there was no need. It didn't bother him that cold grease had settled on top of them. He raked the grease to the side and ate them anyway. I decided his stomach, like the rest of him was must be made of cast iron.

"What took you so long, Son? We waited up for you as long as we could."

"I got a late start," he slurred, directing his attention toward me and trying to avoid any deeper inquiry into his late arrival from his worried mother.

"Baby, did they tell you that I called the school the other day?" Daddy called me Baby, most of the time.

"Yes, the school secretary gave me the message. I...was surprised."

Grandma took out the banana pudding and placed it on the table in front of him. She could see no need to carry on her inquisitions any farther at that time.

"Meryl is doing real good in school. She did good at chopping cotton too. Mrs. Bertram said it took her a little while to figure out the difference between a cotton plant and morning glories, but she soon caught on. Mrs. Bertram said Meryl has made a fine field hand," Grandma rambled nervously.

"Of course, she'd make a fine field hand. She's my little girl, isn't she? Meryl's smart. Did they think she was going to be lazy or couldn't learn how to work in a cotton field?"

He got louder and angrier the longer he spoke. He was easily set off and argumentative when he had been drinking.

Grandma wisely changed the subject. "I have made the extra bed in my bedroom ready for you, Son. Simp helped me make a bedroom for Meryl out of the storage room, so she has her own room now. Do you want to go on to bed? We can talk in the morning."

"Yes, I think I'm ready to get some sleep. I want to get up early and see if Asa Bertram needs a tractor driver. I...won't be going back to my other job," he added casually.

Before leaving the kitchen, he turned around and began digging in his pocket. "Here, Baby, didn't want you to think I forgot your birthday."

He placed a sparkly little charm bracelet in my hand then directed his path toward the bedroom. By this time, the effects of his liquor and lack of sleep didn't allow him to wait for my response. The bracelet was beautiful, but there was not a chance it was going to fit my large wrist. I might have squeezed it on had it been one that would stretch, but this one clasped.

A tear dropped from my cheek onto the small mound of sparkles in my hand. I couldn't have cried enough tears to wash away the stabbing reality that nothing about me was going to fit any normal mold. The bracelet was a sweet gesture from Daddy, but it was a harsh reminder of how disconnected he was to me by thinking such a small piece of jewelry would fit me.

Dismay covered my face as I faintly whispered, "thank you," to an empty doorway.

"Maybe we can add a little length to the chain tomorrow," comforted Grandma, the eternal fixer.

We decided that was not a good time to pursue questions about why he wouldn't be going back to his other job or to tell him my bracelet was too small. That could wait until morning. He might be easier to talk with after a good night's sleep.

His snoring began as soon as his head hit the pillow. It was actually a welcome sound. Despite the fact it sounded as though a bulldozer just moved into the bedroom, it was better than his ranting and raving.

I went to bed thinking that very little had changed with my dad, even if he had made that phone call to my school.

Saturday mornings were wash days when they were not half-days in the fields. My job on wash days was to fill the washer and rinse tubs. It took about seven buckets of rain water for each rinse tub and nearly nine buckets for the washer. Grandma insisted that the clothes be rinsed twice.

If there wasn't enough water in our rain barrel, I would have to finish filling them with well water drawn from the pump on the porch.

Grandma had gotten an early start and filled the washer herself that day so the white clothes could agitate while we ate breakfast. Now all I had to do was fill the rinse tubs. We decided to let Daddy sleep as long as he would; we hoped the longer he slept, the more sober he would be when he awakened.

We were nearly finished with the wash by the time Daddy made his appearance. Grandma gave me instructions to finish hanging the last load of clothes on the line, while she fixed his breakfast.

I came into the kitchen in time to hear him agree to wait until Monday to see if Mr. Bertram needed any extra help. The fields would be empty on Saturday afternoons. That was when everyone headed to town.

If Daddy had been serious about a job, he would have made it his business to get up earlier in the day. "That's just water under the bridge," as Grandma had often been quick to recite. I decided in his case, all that water under a bridge could have possibly caused a flood.

"Come here, Meryl, and give me a hug," Daddy said, while reaching toward me. I had been more eager to do that than I wanted to admit. I'd missed him. He was sober now, and he was the strong, affectionate and humorous dad that I'd always loved.

"So you're doing good in school? Well, I am proud of you," he gloated. "Mom, isn't she a pretty thing? Look at those eyes."

"Hey, you know I saw a woman the other day that was so cross-eyed, when she cried, tears would run down her back?"

That was one of his corny little jokes that Grandma and I had heard many, many times, but we laughed as though we had just heard it for the first time.

"So," he went on, "you're a good field hand? Mom, I knew she would be. This little girl is good at what ever she does. I know the cotton field is hard work, Meryl, but if you keep doing good in school, one day you can choose whatever job you want. My little girl won't have to pick cotton her whole life," he bragged.

Grandma agreed with him quickly as the Bible taught you are to do with your adversaries and went on to ask him what he had been doing while he was away.

He started to squirm. I wasn't sure if it was because of the load of my pudgy frame on his knee or the uncomfortable quizzing from Grandma.

I shifted to a nearby chair. Grandma and I curiously awaited his answer.

"Well, I've been doing odd jobs. I worked at a loading dock for a while, but work got short and they didn't need me any longer."

(*Translation*) He'd probably gotten fired.

"Then, I worked for a while at this garage for this guy, but his business wasn't what it should be; so I moved on."

(*Translation*) He had probably gotten fired there too.

"Then, I worked for a while for this auctioneer but well, I got to missing my little girl here…and you too, Mom."

(*Translation*) He'd probably quit that one.

"Never mind now, I am here, and it is Saturday. How'd you like for us to go to town? We can go in my car and you won't have to crowd in on Simp and Katty," he offered.

I guess that had been the first time it struck me that Grandma and I could have been considered as crowding in on Mr. and Mrs. Simpson. At my old school in Illinois, the kids had teased that I took up too much space on the bench in the lunchroom. My over-sensitivity was starting to show, and being seen as *crowding them* would bother me from that time forward.

"Do you like your bracelet, Baby? I got it at the last auction sale I went to. I wanted to get it for my Baby as soon as I saw it up for bid."

At that point, I could tell that Daddy's heart was in the right place even if his mind wasn't.

"I love it…It so nice, I am going to save it for special occasions. Thank you, Daddy, but my birthday is next Wednesday." Those words hadn't left my mouth before I thought how glad I was that my "thank you" the night before, had fallen upon deaf ears. I couldn't have hid the hurt upon seeing the size of the bracelet. Even if it didn't fit, I didn't want to discourage Daddy's attempts at acknowledging special times for me.

"Well…all right." Grandma interrupted. "Just let me clear the dishes first before we go to town. Meryl can empty the washer and rinse tubs. We *will* be back in time to get the clothes off the line before the dew falls, won't we?"

Grandma would have preferred a little more planning time for that venture but she sure wasn't about to give him any trouble. She was getting a taste of what Mama and I had dealt with when it came to Daddy's barking orders with little or no notice.

I dashed to the porch and started emptying the washer and tubs. Grandma put dishwater on to heat. She was down to the skillets and pans when Daddy decided it was taking too long for his liking. He stood up, came out on the porch, and with little or no effort lifted a half-filled tub of rinse water and emptied it in the drain ditch across the lane. He then turned to Grandma and announced, "It's time to go."

"Can't you finish those pot vessels when you get back home?" he asked. She agreed, but it wasn't Grandma's wish to leave anything unfinished.

The trip to town was fun. Daddy had given us each ten dollars to spend on anything we wanted. That had been nearly as much as I could have made in two days of chopping cotton! He soon disappeared around the corner. We headed to the five and dime, then on to the hardware store for some garden seed.

Grandma had met up with some of her lady friends from church. I plopped down on a nearby bench. Saturday afternoons in town were interesting. Smiles and laughter could be seen and heard from all directions. People were eager to spend their hard earned wages and put the aches and pains of the field behind them for a couple of days. No work was done in the fields on Sundays. I saw Miss Katty and Sadie coming from the Dollar Store. Sadie was licking on a multicolored sucker so large that it practically covered her entire face.

Several men on one end of the street were leaned backward on cane-bottomed chairs, skillfully whittling sticks. A group of women on the other end of the street were jabbering about the entry they had planned for the county fair that year.

Somewhere near the middle of the street, there was a crowd of teenage boys hovering around the window outside the ice cream parlor. A pack of giggly girls were inside swapping stories. The girls flashed just enough come-on smiles to the boys that they too, soon disappeared into the parlor. My eyes were glued. I hoped that before too long, I possibly could be one of those giggly girls.

I caught a familiar name as three men were jay-walking across the street and heading in my direction. Nate McDougal evidently had been up to no good again.

"If his mom will press charges and they can pin it on him, he will be out of the picture for a long time," concluded one of the men.

"I really think that the old woman is scared to death of him but maybe, just maybe this time, he's gone too far," the other man joined in.

The third man was shaking his head in disbelief. "I hear the poor old lady was worked over pretty good. They say he about broke her arm. People better speak up or next time, he could hurt her or someone else even worse; maybe even kill somebody," he stated bluntly.

The first man added, "He ain't right, never has been and I don't see any hope of him gettin' right." They continued picking Nate apart as they walked down the street.

I had begun to put it all together. That was why he was in the back seat of Clete Oller's car. He must have just done something terrible to his poor mother that very day. He hadn't looked too worried as he turned his penetrating eyes toward me again. I felt another one of those creepy chills, just thinking about those evil eyes.

"Meryl, have you seen anything of your dad? It's getting late and I want to get home to get those clothes off the line before the dew falls on them," Grandma asked as she appeared from somewhere behind me.

"No", I said and quickly followed her question with a question.

"Do we have time to get an ice cream cone before we leave?"

My Grandma loved ice cream and candy as much as any child ever could. The suggestion of ice cream made her temporarily forget about Daddy, the clothes on the line, or anything else for the moment. I wanted an ice cream too, but I really just wanted to go into the parlor in hopes the teenagers might still be there.

"I guess we can. It shouldn't take long," she agreed as a tiny smile softened her face. The teenage crowd was gone, but all the chairs were still pulled away of the tables and the juke box was blaring with Elvis singing "Blue Suede Shoes." Grandma couldn't wait to get her ice cream and get out of there. She called juke box music, the devil's music. I was secretly tapping my foot that was hidden under the edge of the counter to the music.

We saw Daddy walking toward us as we left the parlor. He smiled to see the ice creams in our hands and jokingly ask us if we had done about all the damage we could do to that town for the time being. This was his way of letting us know that he was ready to leave.

As we walked toward the car, the smell of liquor on Daddy's breath gave us reason for concern regarding our journey home. Daddy had bragged that since he *drank a lot*, he could hold his liquor better than those who drank only occasionally.

I wondered if we were supposed to find assurance in his assumption that he, being one who *drank a lot, was* safer behind the wheel of a car than those who were only casual drinkers. Guess it sounded good, anyway.

"Mom, did you hear about what that Nate McDougal did to his mother? She's a friend of yours, isn't she?" Daddy asked after we were almost half way home.

Grandma said she hadn't heard of any recent problems with Nate and his mother. I was betting that if she had heard anything, she wouldn't have had any intentions of bringing up Nate McDougal's name to my dad. I knew from his reaction to Nate's name in the past; but didn't know why for sure, but Nate was a definite thorn in Daddy's flesh.

"His mom caught him in her chicken coup and he turned on her again. They say he messed her up pretty bad. She's really bruised up and might have a broken arm and shoulder," he added.

"Oh, no, I hate to hear that. Why, that sweet woman wouldn't hurt anybody. She has had her hands full with that boy since he was born." Grandma was truly sorry for her friend's plight. She and Minnie had something in common in having a son who was a *handful.*

I decided to add what I knew about Nate. "They were talking about Nate in the field, and Miss Katty was upset because he had approached Sadie. And, when he came to our house looking for his dog…"

Daddy never let me finish.

"His dog, he came to your house, Mom? He knows better than to even step a foot in your yard. And with Meryl there now, why I…"

Daddy's face got a deeper shade of red with each word. He was mad and shocked that Grandma hadn't told him that Nate had the gall to come into her yard.

"Now, Larson, he was just looking for his dog." Grandma was trying to put out this spark before it became a full fledged fire.

"But Mr. Bertram said that Sid Carson ran over his dog a few days before." I butted in as I maneuvered my way back into the conversation.

Grandma looked at me with eyes that could have killed. The look in my dad's eyes was nothing short of murderous. I had just added fuel to what was by then an already blazing fire.

"That's it. If I hear of that no account chicken-molesting, perverted, son of a…" Grandma gave him a burning glare and he didn't say what he had really wanted to say. "…bastard, ever stepping a foot in your yard or talking to you or Meryl, or for that matter Sadie either, I will break him in two," he raged!

The longer that conversation went on, the faster my dad drove and the less attention he paid to the road.

"Now, Son, Meryl said she saw him in Clete Oller's car on her way home from school the other day. He's in jail now, where he can't do anymore harm, hopefully for a long time." Grandma's voice was now trembling due to his aggressive demeanor and reckless driving.

"He'd better stay in jail if he knows what's good for him. I mean it, Mom, I'll kill him if he ever touches or does anything to Meryl or you or any of our friends or family."

His booming voice had filled the small car. I shuddered at the echoing words, "I'll kill him...kill him...kill him."

Daddy would have killed Nate McDougal if the wretched man had given him reason to do so. His threats had made me weaken with fear.

"Son, don't talk like that. You scare me and you are scaring Meryl. No one is worth you killing them and getting in trouble for the rest of your life. I'm pretty sure that he'll be in jail for a long time if he did what they're saying he did to his mother."

Her words had not been convincing, even to me. It was evident that we both knew that he would have killed Nate McDougal under the right conditions.

"Well, for his sake, he better stay in jail. That's all I can say." Daddy settled for the last word, and Grandma and I were glad to let him have it.

We finally pulled into the yard. We were safe, but our knees continued to shake as we stepped up on the porch. Daddy made his way directly to the bedroom and went to bed.

Grandma and I rushed to get the clothes off the line. They were still a little bit damp, but she said they could finish drying inside. Truth be known, she had a real problem with clothes hanging on the line on the

Sabbath. That was one of the many rules she had set for herself. Some people took rules and convictions lightly. Rules for Grandma were comparable to not stepping over a line drawn in the sand. It was early for Daddy to go to bed for the night, but we were not about to hinder that happening.

"A good night's sleep will do him good so he can be up early to go and talk with Mr. Bertram," Grandma whispered.

While we were out on the swing before going to bed, she cautioned me to never bring up Nate McDougal's name to Daddy again.

"Grandma, we know Daddy has an awful temper, but did you hear how quickly he got mad tonight at just hearing the name of Nate McDougal?"

"There has been bad blood between your dad and Nate for many years. Larson couldn't prove it, but he had always thought that Nate stole an expensive set of tools from him and probably sold them. The tool box was found floating in Number Eight ditch, but the tools were never found. Larson blamed Nate and not having those tools on missing out on a good job at Terrell Johnson's Gas Station.

He wasn't long out of the army and had just married your mother. Good jobs such as that were not easy to find at that time, especially in these parts.

Y'all moved up north to St. Louis a few years after you were born. He found several pretty good factory jobs, but Larson never liked it if he thought someone got something over on him. You know that for a fact.

He has held a grudge against Nate ever since."

That had been my first time ever hearing that story. It shed some light on why Daddy had so much hatred toward Nate, but I felt it was still a little exaggerated over a set of tools.

We tiptoed to bed. Grandma probably prayed harder that night than usual after hearing Daddy's threats toward Nate.

I covered my ears and tried to shut out the bulldozer before drifting off into a very restless sleep.

Chapter Fourteen

The Mystery Concerning Nate McDougal

J AKE WALBY WAS not a patient man; so we did everything in our power to be ready when he and Effie arrived to take us to church. My dad was noticeably absent from the breakfast table that morning. I checked the porch to see if by chance, he might have been there, but the swing was empty. Reentering the kitchen, I then noticed that the table was set for two.

"Grandma, where's Daddy?"

Clearly troubled, she hesitantly replied, "I don't know, I got up a little earlier than usual to wash up the pot vessels we left soaking yesterday, but he was already gone when I got up. Maybe he has gone to see Mr. Bertram about that tractor job, but it's not likely he'll catch him on a Sunday morning. I figured he'd wait until after they got home from church. He must have been awfully quiet when he got up. I never heard a thing." She was slow to speak, but I could tell her mind was racing with unsettled assumptions.

"He'll probably be home before long. It's not like him to miss breakfast," I tried to console.

It wasn't a written law at her house or even a matter of discussion, but there was a mutual understanding of sorts, concerning each other's whereabouts. Neither of us went anywhere without announcing to the other that she was going. It wasn't out of demand but out of consideration. Grandma and I didn't even make a trip to the *out-house,* unless we told the other one we were going. Courtesy not being one of his major attributes, I supposed Daddy didn't think the *rules* applied to him.

"Put the butter and jelly on the table. We're about ready to sit down. Jake will be here before we know it. We sure don't want to rub him the wrong way, or he'll be grumpy all the way to church."

I was thinking this trip to church wouldn't be any different than all of the others had been, but I did as she requested.

It usually took about a half hour to forty five minutes to get to Hayti, and church, but if we had to make the trip with a grumpier than usual somebody, it would have seemed like an eternity.

Church was a welcome outlet for me. Interacting with the church kids, even if only on Sundays was better than not at all. Also, I was never the butt of any of their jokes about size. And of course, everyone was always anxious for me to sing.

I noticed Grandma slipping her hand up when Bro. Gayle asked for unspoken prayer requests. God and I knew what that was all about for sure. She was forever asking Him to keep a watchful eye on Daddy.

While on our way back home, I tried to be out of sight, out of mind, as Grandma chatted with Jake and Effie. While I focused on the watery furrows in the rain-soaked fields as we whisked by, I continued to have perplexing visions of being stuck up to my knees in the gumbo mud.

A sickness rolled in the pit of my stomach. No matter how many times that I tried to erase them, the visions continued to flash. How silly, here I was in a dry car, wearing my new pointed-toe girl shoes, and all I could think about was being stuck in the middle of a muddy cotton field. Then, I realized, strangely enough, how similar those visions were to my haunting dream.

The wail of a siren startled me and overpowered the visions. The sheriff's patrol car zipped by at a pace faster than usual. Trying to determine the cause of the commotion made Effie, Jake, and Grandma lose their train of thought. They picked up where they left off, once the car had passed.

"I tell you that church spends too much money on the youth. It is like us older folks don't even count. It is the youth this and the youth that. It makes me not even want to put any money in the plate when they send it around."

Jake didn't like not having a say in every decision made in the church. The new pastor and his family had a fresh approach concerning church programs and projects, and Jake didn't like change of any kind.

I was guessing what Grandma said about Jake's nose

was probably true. I once commented about him having the longest nose I had ever seen on a person. She said it probably grew longer every time he stuck it into things he shouldn't have. He'd best watch it; from the way this conversation was going, it was liable to grow even longer still, before we got home that day.

"Jeannie." Jake decided to call me Jeannie since that was my church name. "Why aren't you saying anything? You never seem to have much to say." He had me focused in his rear-view mirror as he usually did when he was driving.

It was evident from the silence in the car, that it must be my turn to speak.

I was saved from having to respond. Before I could reply, another police car flew by.

The conversation immediately went to "what on earth could be going on to call for two police cars heading somewhere in such a hurry." Fortunately, this line of conversation continued for most of the rest of our trip home.

We finally turned the corner and arrived at our house. I was relieved to be spared from defending the youth of the church and our new pastor's approach.

"Y'all have a good dinner now, Mrs. Strom. Didn't I see Larson home?" Effie wedged in the question, before Grandma could make it out of the car.

"Yes, he came home Friday evening. He's going to stay around these parts for a while I think. He misses Meryl Jean. Poor thing, he's lost without Edna. I don't think he really knows what to do with himself."

Grandma was answering all the way out the door, trying not to leave an opening for more questions concerning details of my dad's plans. We truthfully didn't have details. We were not sure what he was going to do. Maybe he would be home, and we could ask where he was that could have been more important than breakfast.

Once inside, we found an empty house with no sign of Daddy's return during our absence. We changed from our church clothes. Grandma started dinner and instructed me to 'fetch' a bucket of water.

I was really glad that Mr. Simpson had repositioned the pump on the porch. It wasn't nearly so far to carry a full bucket of water from the porch as it would have been from out in the yard.

Just as I reached for the bucket bale, Daddy appeared from around the corner of the house. We both flinched at seeing each other. He leaped on the porch and grabbed the bucket bail.

"Where were you, Daddy? Grandma said you were gone when she got up this morning." I might have seen how much trouble he was having with my question, if I'd been looking at his face.

He wasn't as fortunate as he entered the kitchen. Grandma asked him the same question, and she was looking straight at him.

"I...well...I had trouble sleeping so I drove around a little bit. I...ran into Deke McCrady, you know, Asa Bertram's son-in-law. He was home from St. Louis for the weekend and was having car trouble, so I stopped to help him. He said he thinks Asa needs someone to repair a few pieces of machinery he has broken down. Maybe he might want me to look at them."

He added that Deke's wife gave him breakfast in payment for his good deed. His answer satisfied Grandma on two counts: one, he accounted for his whereabouts, and two, he had eaten. He barely got the words out of his mouth before we heard Simp, Katty, and Sadie stomp up on the porch.

"Mrs. Strom, did you hear what happened?" Miss Katty expounded as she stormed into the kitchen. "They found Nate McDougal's body floating in Number Eight ditch!"

"Oh, my Lord," Grandma gasped, "his poor mother. I need to go see if I can help her." Suddenly a big hiss came from the stove. The potatoes were boiling over, and Grandma rushed to the rescue.

"We hear she is at the hospital where they took her right after they found Nate. She was already weak from where he…beat the poor thing. People are saying he worked her over again, maybe broke her nose this time. I'm not surprised that someone killed him. Everyone knows what a wicked person he was." There was no sympathy from Miss Katty for sure.

"I thought he was in jail. Meryl saw him in Clete Oller's patrol car on her way home from school Friday afternoon," Grandma said in disbelief, after setting the potatoes aside.

"He escaped; looks like they underestimated him at that jail. He was smart enough to outsmart them," Mr.

Simpson grunted.

"That must have been where the police cars were going in such a hurry when they passed us on our way home from church." I added.

I then noticed that my dad hadn't had a word to say about Nate's death. Grandma must have had the same thought.

"Larson, did you hear any thing about this?" We all turned to see and hear his reply to Grandma's question. Surely if he'd known, he would have already said something.

"No...this is the first I've heard...Simp, did you hear how he died? Do they have any information on how it happened?"

It was a little odd to hear Daddy engage in conversation with Simp. He and Simp didn't have a lot of interaction. They were two different personalities. Simp was a reserved and quiet man that usually stayed in the background. Some people labeled him as timid.

Daddy was a bold, outspoken leader of the pack. He was anything but timid. It was not that they actually disliked each other; they just didn't have much in common. Truth be known, Simp resented my dad's escapades and the added stress they put on his good friend and neighbor. He loved my Grandma like a son himself. Daddy thought of Simp as not a manly man and as what some referred to as *hen-pecked*.

Nonetheless, I didn't doubt for a minute that anyone who became the least bit threatening to a friend or neighbor of Grandma's would have found a big fist and a lot of muscle to contend with. That was a fact. I also knew Daddy's fist and muscle would probably have been a force to be reckoned with, even if anyone was crazy enough to kick a friend's dog.

"They say his neck was broken and he had some teeth missing. Come to think of it, I think he already had teeth missing; anyway, they say there was no sign of a struggle." Mr. Simpson's answer to Daddy's question and report of Nate McDougal's demise was totally cold and matter-of-fact. If I hadn't known better, there wasn't a clue that he had been talking about a once living, breathing human being.

"There is no telling who did this. That man had so many people who despised him; there were probably people standing in line to kill him. I hate it for his mother to lose a son, but I say *good riddins!*" There was no doubt that Miss Katty felt little if any grief for the dead man.

As for me, all I could remember were his eyes. Those eyes looked up, down, and through me. Now, they saw nothing. I was ashamed and hated to admit it, but I too felt a sense of relief that he was no longer a threat. The mere mention of his name could bring about all kinds of emotions, mostly disgust and hatred.

At thirteen, I had dealt with the deaths of three people I knew personally: Grandpa Omar, who had died one year before my mother; my mother, the most painful death of all; and now Nate McDougal. Well…in Nate's case, I knew only his eyes. He was less than a human being to some, but a child to a mother whose unconditional love for him outweighed the heavy burden he presented her.

THE NEXT MORNING, Daddy took the job with Mr. Bertram. If he didn't have such a drinking problem and bad temper, Daddy could be an asset to almost anyone. He was a good tractor driver and, unlike a lot of others, could also fix the unpredictable things, when they broke down. This job meant we might have my dad with us for a little while at least.

"How about I drop you off at school this morning?" Daddy offered. Didn't I feel special? I could be dropped off at the entrance like the McCrady girls.

I talked all the way, telling Daddy about how I liked this school much better than any I had ever gone to before. We pulled around the circle drive leading to the entrance. As I reached for the door handle, Daddy slipped me two quarters.

"It's for dinner today," he said. I gave him a hug and a peck, thanked him for the ride and the quarters; then rushed to meet up with Polly. I decided against telling him my plan of not eating in the school cafeteria. He'd probably say I was being silly and should have ignored any unwanted remarks.

A lot he knew. I tried that in Illinois, and it didn't work. No, I wasn't going to give anyone a chance to start with the insults, and maybe it wouldn't happen. I had no intention of letting it happen!

If we hurried, Polly and I could quiz each other for our first hour test. She was an excellent student. I had become a pretty good one myself. I asked her the questions first, and by the time we were through, I knew all the answers as well as she did. Then, she asked me, and we were doubly prepared. We almost always earned perfect scores on our tests, and we hoped today would be no exception.

Come noon, Polly and I headed to the Big Store café, called *The Green Fly*. I always thought it took someone with a warped sense of humor to name a cafe, The *Green Fly* and expect people to want to eat there.

I was wrong. The *Green Fly* was one of the busiest places in Muddy Ox. It didn't hurt matters that it was the *only* cafe in town, or that a hamburger and a coke were just a quarter.

There were two doors to the café. Most patrons used the main door leading off the sidewalk. I insisted that we use the Big Store entrance and go through the swinging doors located in the back of the store to get to the café. That allowed me to check out how many students were there before we actually went in. If there were too many, Polly could order our food.

Arriving at the store, we climbed the nine long narrow steps that lined the entire front porch and entered through the wide double doors. The wooden floors creaked with each step as we tracked down the aisles, toward the back entrance to *The Green Fly*.

Inside, the store, we were greeted with the rich

leathery smell of saddles, boots, and belts before getting to the unpleasant odors of fertilizer and sprays. A display of cotton sacks ranging from a child's five foot, to an accomplished picker's fourteen foot, hung along the left wall.

The clothing section was to the far right. The canned food, hardware, drug store and dry good sections were aisled in between. A variety of just about anything and everything could be found within the confines of the Big Store.

Just as we pushed past the swinging doors, Tara and four other cheerleaders bounced through the front entrance. Several jocks were sitting in a corner booth. Melly and a group of her friends were at a table in the other corner. I slipped the quarters into Polly's hand for her to do the ordering.

The clerk passed Polly our sack of food, and we grabbed our cokes. I quietly followed her out the main café door to the store's small back porch. There we shared our tasty feast in seclusion. It doesn't matter how drastic that may have appeared; I was desperate to avoid giving anyone ammunition to taunt me.

"That was nice of your dad to give you money today for dinner. Does he know you're not eating at the school cafeteria?" Polly asked while she savored her burger.

"I think he just assumed I'm eating there. I am not about to tell him that I'm not. He wouldn't understand anyway. He would just say for me to ignore the stares and teasing. He has no idea. No one would dare tease him about anything. They'd be afraid to try. I bet it never occurred to him that unless he gives me money like today, Grandma doesn't have money for me to eat every day anyway. Daddy doesn't think that far ahead about things like that."

"I haven't told you this, but Mrs. Pendergrass took me aside the other day and said an anonymous person had offered to pay for me to eat at the cafeteria for the rest of the year if I wanted to." Polly confided.

"What did you say? Hey, don't worry about me. I wouldn't want to eat there if we had all kinds of money. All of my reasons for not eating dinner there are not the same as yours."

"I told her no, but not just because you don't eat there. Of course, I would rather be with you than eat anywhere else with the others anyway. I just wouldn't feel right to eat a good dinner meal every day when my brothers and sisters have to do without. I didn't tell her that for fear she would think I was hinting that someone pay for their meals also. I'm just fine and they are just fine too. But, if anyone got their meals paid for, I would want it to be them. It was a nice gesture, but we are all not going to starve to death. My mother has a meal cooked for us every night."

I thought that was highly unselfish of Polly. It reinforced why she and I were such good friends.

Gym class was immediately after noon hour. Despite Polly being the thin one, I was the more athletic. My physical activity was not hindered by my size. I was built solid, and my weight was evenly distributed. I had good, strong leg and arm muscles. I was a fair basketball player and could move up and down the gym floor with ease.

Coach Webb divided us into teams. I was assigned a guard position on my team. Although winning or losing didn't constitute a grade, we girls were quite competitive.

It was down to the last few minutes of the game. Hezzie Plum, an opponent on the other team, came barreling down the court, in hopes of making the last shot. I was in position for successfully blocking her. The whistle blew. The game was over. We won.

Hezzie was annoyed that her shot could have won the game and I was what kept her from making it. She gathered quite a crowd with her antics.

"What do you expect with her out there? Who can get around that fat thing? Hey, Fatso, next time stay out of my way."

Hezzie's words echoed throughout the open gymnasium, and the word Fatso seemed to get louder as it bounced from wall to wall, filling the entire room.

What happened next was one of those once-in-a-lifetime unexplainable occurrences. I would never know for sure how I was able to do what I did and could probably have never done it again! While I was standing in the upper far right corner of half court, Hezzie was in the lower far left corner. I turned, lobbed the ball and hit her squarely in the middle of the back of her head. I started walking toward her as soon as the ball left my hand. She turned around, and we were nose to nose.

You could have heard a pin drop at that point.

Hands on my hips, standing flat-footed, I began.

"My name is Jean, Jean Strom. If you don't want to call me Jean, then don't call me anything."

I was not sure if it was the authoritative tone in my voice, the look in my eyes, the expression on my face, or the throbbing in the back of her head, but she never said a word back to me. Nor did anyone else in the crowd say anything.

Hezzie turned, threw the ball down, and walked off. Her crowd lingered briefly trying to grasp what had just happened, then followed her into the locker room.

I picked up the ball and tossed it into the bin. Polly, the remainder of the group, and I filed into the locker room in silence. No one discussed the previous occurrence. That was the first and the last time I was ever called an abusive name in that school.

Once we were alone, Polly declared, "Jean, I don't think I have ever seen anything like that before. How did you make that ball hit her in the back of her head like that?" Polly was amazed, and to tell you the truth, so was I, as we discussed the phenomenon on the way to our next class.

"I don't know how I did that. I never looked or aimed the ball, while turning and lobbing it toward her. It was like a guided missile hitting its target. I am going to feel like my guardian angel was at work again."

Polly understood because I had previously shared my other two guardian angel episodes with her.

"Well, it was scary. What would you have done if

she'd said something back to you or started a fight?"

"I am not sure. I guess I would have fought if I had needed to. Polly, you don't know how awful it is to have people make fun of you like I have. You're thin; you have small feet and can wear normal shoes. I just can't allow it to start."

She sensed my pain. "Jean, I have been made fun of because we move around all the time and also, because my mom and dad have such a large family. I don't have the nicest clothes or hardly ever have spending money.

If some kids want to make fun of you, they will find a reason. Anyway, I don't think you will ever have to worry about Hezzie crossing you again or for that matter, anyone who witnessed that scene."

"I hope not, I don't know what I can do to top that." I said laughingly as we walked down the hall toward class.

News got around quickly in such a small school. Tara caught up with me on our way home. Of course, she had heard every detail, but she wanted to hear it again from me.

"I am glad you put Hezzie in her place. She's never been a good sport and is always smarting off to everyone."

It was good to hear Tara being supportive. She was popular, part of the *in-crowd*, and she was a good one to have in my corner.

I told Grandma and Daddy the story that evening, during supper, and Grandma verbally worried about every part of it. She worried that Hezzie could have been injured. What if she had turned around and the ball had hit her in the face? Was I going to get in trouble at school?

Daddy reminded her that not any of that had happened or was likely to. He boasted that it would teach anyone not to mess with his little girl. He added that maybe Hezzie might think next time before she opened her mouth. He assured Grandma that if I was going to get in trouble, it would have probably already happened. He figured that Hezzie would have gotten in trouble herself for what she said. He also promised he would take care of it, if I did get in trouble.

Now there was a troublesome thought. My dad going to the school and turning it upside down was the last thing I wanted. Talk about bringing unwanted attention to my being made fun of for being fat.

No, somehow Daddy should never find out if I did get in trouble. I wouldn't have shared it with him at all if I had thought that through.

My worries were for nothing. I never heard another word about our gym encounter. In fact, Hezzie and I became good friends after that. Polly said she probably thought I was someone she would want on her side if there had to be sides.

From then on, if Hezzie was appointed captain of a team, I was one of the first people she picked. We never had another cross word, and I was glad.

I learned an important lesson that day. Sometimes, I was going to have to face my enemies head on. I was anything but a bully or a tough guy like my dad, but maybe some of his genes did surface to give me whatever courage I needed at the right time. Hey, it could even have been some of my mom's genes. Whatever it was... I was glad I had it!

Chapter Fifteen

The Arm of the Law
Reaches for Answers

W ORD ABOUT NATE McDougal's demise spread like a field on fire. According to the coroner's report, he had died from a single blow, instantly breaking his neck; however, the authorities were unable to determine the murder weapon.

Nate's mother was hospitalized, recovering from broken ribs and trauma-induced shock. Most residents of Muddy Ox were eager to voice an opinion about who could have possibly saved our little community from the misery caused by one Nate McDougal.

Effie Walby heard from a very reliable source, that our local sheriff's department was working closely with a big city detective from Springfield in hopes of solving the case. Everyone was eager to tell what they knew, heard, or thought about Nate.

Daddy was still with us. We were expecting any day for him to get the traveling itch, but so far, he was staying put.

That evening found him working late to get Asa Bertram's tractor ready for plowing the next day. We'd had our supper, and his was waiting for him on the stove. My homework finished, I joined Grandma out in the swing to wait for him.

Suddenly a long, shiny black sedan pulled into our yard. Its length filled the entire parking space by the garage. A tall, dark-haired man wearing a black hat and business suit slid from beneath the wheel, locked his car, and strolled over to the porch. I thought it strange that he locked his car when it was parked in our yard, in broad daylight. Grandma later attributed that to the mistrust that big-city people had for almost everyone.

"Evening, ladies, I am Private Detective Forest Desmond from Springfield."

He flashed his badge upon reaching the porch. Never looking up from the stack of papers he was shuffling, he addressed Grandma in a cold and impersonal manner, "You, Miz Alice Strom?"

"Yes, I am. I am Alice Strom." Grandma was annoyed and thought it rude if someone didn't look at the person to which he was talking.

"You have a son named Larson Strom?" the officer continued.

"Yes, he isn't home right now. He's working for Mr. Asa Bertram down the road. I expect him home shortly."

Her snappy brown eyes burned right through this man as she awaited his next question.

"And who's this young lady?" he asked.

"This is Meryl, Larson's daughter. She lives here with me."

He nodded then went back to sifting through his papers. I was guessing whoever I was wasn't of much importance to him.

"Mind then if I sit and wait if you're expecting Larson soon?"

He abruptly took a seat on the edge of the porch without waiting for her response—another act of rudeness as far as Grandma was concerned. She had been expecting him or someone like him after receiving Effie's inside information; so his visit was not a total surprise. However, he didn't know that he had already irritated Grandma twice, and I wasn't sure how much longer she would tolerate his behavior without letting him know it.

"Can you tell me how I can get in touch with John and Katelina Simpson? I was told they live around here." he questioned.

It was odd to hear anyone refer to Miss Katty, by her real name. I now knew why she went by Katty. Her real name didn't fit her at all! She was anything but a fragile, frilly, little Katelina.

Grandma was ready to tell him they lived next door when the pair appeared around the corner with Sadie following not far behind.

"These are my friends, John and Katty Simpson and their daughter, Sadie. They live next door."

Mr. Simpson extended his hand in greeting to the Detective, while Miss Katty offered him a cold stare.

The officer smiled at Sadie, but was met with a frown. Sadie had been allowed to react to people in whatever manner she saw fit. There was no denying that she saw fit *not* to like this man.

"I'm Private Detective Forest Desmond, from Springfield. I'm here to investigate the Nathaniel McDougal incident. Mind if I ask you folks some questions?"

Mr. Simpson nodded in agreement. I gave Miss Katty my seat on the swing. Grandma asked me to drag a couple of chairs out of the kitchen for Simp and the Detective, but Mr. Simpson said there'd no need. I got the impression he didn't intend for that inquisition to last very long. He perched himself on the edge of the porch and leaned comfortably against the post. Sadie and I sat like little mice with big ears.

"How well did you folks know Mr. Nathaniel McDougal?" the officer began.

"I didn't know him very well a'tall. Didn't know his name was Nathaniel for that part. Few people knew him well or even called him friend. No one called him Mister." Simp volunteered.

"He didn't deserve to be called Mister," Miss Katty spouted.

With her remark, Detective Desmond took the opportunity to direct the next question to her. "It is evident he didn't have many friends. I can see he wasn't high on your list. It is one thing for people not to like him. Do you know anyone who would want to kill him?" The detective squarely met her gaze.

Surprisingly, Miss Katty seemed a little intimidated, something I had never seen from her before. She quickly regained her composure and the intimidation was short-lived.

"Hmmm well… I'm not sure about who would want to kill him, but everyone was afraid he was goin' to kill his own mother if he wasn't stopped."

She shifted the topic back to Nate and his abuse to his mother, where she thought it belonged.

"Is that a fact? Yes, well, you're not the first person who has told me about how he treated his family. You think that'd be enough to cause someone outside the family to want to kill him?" He asked as he continued directing his attention toward Miss Katty.

It was an angry Mr. Simpson who delivered his answer. "Want to, probably. Now, actually kill him; that's a different story. No one wants to see a poor helpless woman be hurt."

"Do you think he could do enough to make either you or your wife kill him?" questioned the officer.

"I have never laid a hand on anyone in my life." Mr. Simpson hardly let the officer get the words out of his mouth before he blurted his angry response.

"I have an account from several people who were present, along with you and your wife, in a cotton field, belonging to a Mr. Asa Bertram, who state that they overheard you and your wife, Katelina here, threaten to kill Nathanial McDougal."

Miss Katty jumped to her feet while the accusing words were still rolling out of his mouth.

"Now, you look here, you Mr. highfalutin big-city-man. We didn't kill that ornery, no good, chicken molesting fool. We only said that because we were told he was messing around our Sadie. Now, if he had got to Sadie, we would have killed him and been glad of it. We didn't kill Nate, but we are not bothered because someone else did."

With that said, Simp and Katty stood, gathered Sadie, and all stomped off together.

Sadie turned to look at the offender as they were leaving. The only thing missing from the scowl on her face was an extended tongue. Detective Desmond was fortunate to have been spared that gesture. It was one that Sadie resorted to quite often.

Grandma saw that didn't go well for her friends. If that man didn't already suspect them, he did after that episode. No doubt he probably suspected Miss Katty!

"Detective Desmond, you will have to overlook Simp and Katty. They are very straightforward with their opinions. Especially Katty, and especially when it involves their baby girl, Sadie. They're overly protective of her, as I'm sure you could tell.

They are not, although it may have sounded that way, violent people. Katty might talk a little rough, but I don't feel that she has it in her to kill another human being. The only thing I can think of that would push her that far is if someone actually did hurt Sadie."

"Evidently, they thought Nate was a threat to their daughter. Mrs. Simpson said she'd kill him if he had gotten to Sadie."

"Well…that didn't happen. Nate only talked to Sadie about his dog, he never touched her. It's a sure thing that someone killed Nate McDougal, but I can promise you, that it wasn't my long-time friends and neighbors, John Simpson or his wife Katty. They were with Larson, Meryl, and me in town all afternoon and way up until Saturday evening," Grandma said continuing to defend her friends.

"I can assure you, until I find out who the real killer is, the Simpsons are suspects," Desmond promised.

"I was aware of when they came home. Meryl and me were sitting out here on the swing, after Larson went to sleep, and we heard them getting Sadie ready for bed. We live rather close to each other, and as you probably noticed, Katty speaks in a pretty loud voice. She is easily heard from our house.

"Tell me again, what time it was when you all got home?" The detective wanted to see if all the stories were consistent.

Grandma was tired of repeating the same thing over and over, but if she could get Simp and Katty off this guy's list, she'd do it, however many times it was needed.

"We got home around seven-thirty that night. Simp and Katty pulled in a little after that. By nine or so, it was quiet and we had all gone to bed, just as I had already told you."

Grandma tried to do what came naturally to her; put a little *healing oil* on the situation.

"So you are sure your friends are not involved in

Nate's death and you can vouch for the time they arrived home?"

"Yes, I already have, but will do it again, if you insist," Grandma was quick to pledge.

"What about your son, Larson? I've heard several accounts from people in these parts about him. It would seem there were few people who feared *Nate* any more than they do Larson. Seems he has had problems with *Nate* for many years. Those I spoke with state that Larson has an explosive temper."

This man surely seemed determined to place the blame for Nate's death on either Grandma's son or her friends. She was primed to answer when my dad broke in instead. He had overheard the accusations as he approached. His face was crimson red. It was hard to tell if it was red from anger or sun exposure.

Because I knew him so well and by the set of his jaw, I would have betted on anger.

Daddy's voice was deeper than usual, as he slowly pitched questions toward this intruder. "Tell me, since when is it a crime to have a temper? Do you have a temper, Sir? You have asked everyone else in this town something about me. Now, here I am, ask me for yourself."

There was no sign the lawman made any ripples at all into my dad's stream of confidence. Now, it was the detective's turn to be intimidated. If anyone could bring this about, Daddy could.

Detective Desmond was caught by surprise. He didn't expect Daddy to appear in this manner. I imagined it was shocking to be face to face with this bigger-than-life personality he had been told so much about.

"Larson Strom?" his voice was steadier now that he regained a bit more control.

"If you don't mind, sir, I'd like to ask you a few questions concerning your whereabouts between the evening and morning hours of the day of Nathanial McDougal's death." The detective plunged on with renewed confidence.

"I was in Kennett with my mom and daughter. I went to bed right after we got home that night," Daddy gave a straight answer to a straight question.

"Are there others who can attest to seeing you in Kennett that day?" Desmond continued.

"Yes, our neighbors the Simpsons can. For that matter, Sheriff Clete Oller and I had a few beers together at The Bottoms Up Bar. Uhh... He was off duty, of course. There were several others there too, want me to name them all?" Daddy felt pretty smug, having a member of the law as an alibi.

"No... No, that'll do. I can speak with Mr. Oller myself. So, you came home and went right to bed. Is there anyone other than your mother or daughter who can confirm that?"

If he had been looking at Daddy and not his notes, he possibly would have seen what Grandma and I saw in my dad's face with that question.

Daddy slowly strolled over to the porch and sat, then continued, "Like I said, I had a few drinks with Mr.

Oller and a few more before that. I am not accustomed to interrupting a perfectly good night's sleep, especially when I've had a little alcohol to help me with it."

"Do you plan to be around these parts for a while, just in case I might have any more questions?" the officer queried.

"I don't have any plans of going anywhere right now. I have a few jobs to do for Asa Bertram before pickin' season gets here."

As he rose to his feet, Daddy used his body language to signal it was time for that interrogation to end. Taking the hint, the detective bade us farewell, collected his paperwork, and headed to his car. If his behavior wasn't foreign enough to us, he lingered briefly, and stooped down by the open door of his car. It looked as though he had a camera and was taking a picture of the ground for some reason. Puzzling as his behavior was, we were just glad for him to leave. A cloud of dust trailed behind as the detective's car raced down the gravel road. Daddy turned toward the kitchen door, but Grandma gave him a look that stopped him in his tracks.

"What?" Daddy knew she had concerns.

"I didn't say anything, but you know you were gone when I got up that next morning. I'd like to know where you were and what you were doing." That was a demand from his mother and not a request.

"I…I woke up with a headache, I guess I had a little too much to drink the night before and I… went for a ride." His answer might have sufficed had we not seen his previous reaction to the detective's questioning.

"Son, I didn't lie to that man. I am just glad he didn't ask me point blank, if I could say you were here all night. You know I'll not lie about anything. I'd feel more satisfied if you'd give me a little better explanation as to where you went when you took your early morning ride." Daddy's mother was clearly perplexed by his excuse.

"Remember, I told you I ran into Deke McCrady, worked on his car, then had breakfast with them? Mom, I can promise you, I had nothing to do with Nate McDougal's death. I am glad someone did him in, and I am almost sorry to say that it wasn't me, but I didn't do it." He sure sounded convincing.

"Well, you had best not be saying that to anyone. Katty almost got herself in hot water with her honesty about Nate's death." It seemed that Grandma was appeased for the moment. I supposed I was too.

"Mom, you know as well as I do that you can't count on both hands and feet, the people who hated that poor excuse of a man. That big old city investigator will be here a long time trying to get to the bottom of this if he plans to question each one of them."

Daddy was right. Detective Desmond would be hard pressed to find anyone in the entire town who didn't have a problem with Nate McDougal or didn't dislike him intensely.

My bed offered little solace that night. Desmond's description of how Nate McDougal's broken body was found lying in Number Eight ditch continued to appear.

I couldn't erase the mental picture of his lanky, lifeless frame, partly submerged with waves of dirty ditch water lapping around it. I could imagine the unruly curl that always found its way down his forehead and seemed to parallel the unruliness of his miserable life. Then...I remembered his eyes before drifting off to sleep.

I worried about that detective and if he was going to uncover anything that would link my dad to Nate's murder.

Sleep eventually came, and so did the recurring dream that had troubled me most of my life. Once more, I had become stuck in the mud and couldn't pull free and began screaming and crying. Next, I was on my mother's lap as she frantically wiped my face, trying to cleanse me of mud. As usual, I woke up in a sweat, terrified, my heart pounding within my chest. After much tossing and turning, sleep returned. The dream was gone again, at least for a while.

Chapter Sixteen

My Battle with Stinging Worm

THE EXTREMELY HOT summer produced a sea of fluffy, white cotton in every field, giving the farmers high hopes for a profitable yearly yield. This was the last week of school before picking season began. We students would be dismissed to help harvest the crops. I couldn't wait!

The McCrady girls continued to promise there was more money to be made picking cotton than could be made chopping it. They also warned me again about it being harder work. Remembering my blister and walking on those hard, gumbo clods, I couldn't imagine it being any worse. How hard could it be? You pulled the cotton from the pods and stuffed it into the sacks. When your sack was full, you weighed and emptied it. You collected your money at the end of the week. It sounded simple enough to me.

Polly and I said our good-byes for the summer. Our paths never crossed during the weeks of harvest time.

Because neither of us had phones; we couldn't call. Grandma and I didn't have a car. Her family didn't have gas money to go visiting. We didn't expect to see or hear from each other again until school started back. She'd picked cotton before; so there were no surprises in store for her. It was just another harvest as far as she was concerned. She hoped her dad wouldn't find a new crop to follow and move her and her family away. The farmer that her dad was sharecropping for was saying he might need him year around and talked as though his job could evolve into a permanent one. She prayed that was true so she could graduate with our class, especially me, her new best friend.

It was barely dawn as I headed for the end of the road to catch the Bertram's tractor-drawn wagon. Starting early was a must while the dew was still on the cotton to help with the morning weight. However, there was a fine line for how soon the field boss would let us start our day's work. It was one thing for the cotton to be a little damp and another for it to be dripping wet.

The girls and I had brand new, nine-foot sacks to begin the season with. Most of the men used twelve to even fourteen foot sacks, but Grandma decided a nine-foot sack was plenty long enough for me to start out with. I was also wearing a new pair of work jeans, a long sleeve denim shirt and of course, a new bonnet. Gloves were a nuisance for picking cotton. They hung on the sharp burrs, making it nearly impossible to get all the cotton out of the pods. They considerably slowed the process in which speed was a must, so there'd be no gloves for me.

Once off the wagon, we were directed to wait until the dew level was right. When we were allowed to begin, Tara and I chose rows next to each other. Melly and Scarlett's rows were on the other side of Tara's. It wasn't long before I fell behind. Mrs. Bertram picked ahead to help me catch up.

"Jean, you have to keep both hands working at the same time. Keep feeding the cotton into your sack and pack it down good to make room for more. Get it all, pick it clean and don't leave a sloppy row. They knock the price down at the gin if the load is *dirty* with leaves, burrs, or half-opened bolls. We can't take dirty cotton to the gin." The girls said she would have made a good drill sergeant; I agreed.

I soon saw what they meant by harder. First of all, the heavier the sack got, the deeper it dug into my shoulder. After about an hour of picking bent over, my back felt nearly broken when I tried to stand up straight.

I experimented with trying to pick while crawling on my knees to give my back a rest for a while, like I saw some of the others doing. Before long, my knees were red and hurting. The pace was much slower; so there was nothing to do but resort to bending over again.

The sun was pounding down with full force. I wiped the sweat that was now running down into my eyes, with the sleeve of my shirt. The extreme heat had dried and hardened the burrs so that their points were as sharp as needles. The trick was to get the cotton out without jabbing the burr points into your fingers. I was not very successful with that maneuver.

Soon, every finger I had was bleeding and I was humorously wondering if the dripping blood might have made my cotton weigh heavier. Mrs. Bertram never said anything about blood. I forged ahead, trying to reach the end of the row with as much cotton packed in my sack as possible while leaving as little as I could on the stalks behind.

Daddy was still working for Mr. Bertram. I could see him on the tractor in the field next to us. It was comforting that at least I knew where he was most of the time.

Suddenly, I felt a sharp, burning, sting on the top of my right hand. I soon discovered the culprit was a large stinging worm, still clinging to a leaf on the stalk I had just picked. The worms were the same shade of green as the leaves; so it was easy to brush against one without notice. My offender left a welt on my hand about three inches long and an inch wide. Letting out a gasp from the pain, I couldn't hide the tears that rolled down my hot cheeks.

Instantly, a grubby stub of a hand grabbed my arm and slapped a wet chaw of tobacco on my sting. I was so shocked I hardly had time to think about what had just happened or who had come to my rescue. I wasn't sure if given a choice, I would have chosen the stinky, wet, wad of chewed tobacco over the sting of the worm. That was, until I realized that my pain was gone and the redness and swelling had lessened.

It was then that I saw how dirty and unkempt my

rescuer was. Everything about him was dirty. His hair was shaggy. His shoes were ragged and run over. His shirt had rivers of tobacco juice stains running down it that were surely the accumulation of more than only one day's chewing. It was impossible to distinguish if the stench of him was from the lack of body hygiene, bad breath, or perspiration mixed with fresh tobacco drippings.

I had never seen this person before, but that was not out of the ordinary. There were often several groups of migrant workers brought to the field by various contractors. There were also many sharecroppers, such as Polly's dad, who when they got their fields caught up, would work for other farmers to make a little extra money. It was not often you knew every single person in the field.

"You're Lars's girl aren't you?" I was surprised to hear he knew my dad. He knew him well enough to call him Lars as did most of his other friends. I was even more surprised he knew I was his daughter.

"Yes," I said reluctantly.

"I know your dad from a business deal. I saw you with him in town the other day; name's Obe Stone. Those worms can be mean and ornery, can't they?" He reached in his shirt pocket for a fresh chaw of tobacco, since his previous one had found a new purpose.

"Something wrong here?" Daddy inquired as he suddenly appeared from behind us.

"Just saw your little girl being attacked by this monster cotton worm," Obe said as he broke off the stalk housing the worm, shook him to the ground, then stomped him into oblivion.

Daddy gave Obe a lingering gaze, then turned to me, "You all right?"

"I'm better now," I sobbed. "This man put some tobacco on it, and it doesn't sting any longer."

"Thanks, Obe, she's new at this field hand stuff." Daddy gave the worm another stomp and ground the worm deeper into the sod, as to not be outdone by his friend.

"Just happened to be at the right place at the right time, Lars," He said with a mysterious smile on his face.

"It's better than being in the wrong place at the wrong time, am I right, Obe?"

They exchanged glares for a few seconds; then Obe turned and headed back to his row and nearly filled cotton sack. "Be seeing you around." He said as he harnessed his sack and started picking again.

As we watched him pick his way on down his row, he glanced back once more and gave my dad a half-hearted salute.

"He says he knows you from a business deal and he saw us in town. Who is he Daddy?"

Don't worry your pretty little head about him. He is an ok guy, but he's a nobody. He's just a man I talked to about a dog. I've got to get back to my tractor, and you need to catch up now. Keep a look-out for those worms, ok?" Daddy went back to work, and Mrs. Bertram came to help me catch up once more.

My sack was nowhere near full when it was time for

the girls to go weigh theirs, but I shouldered it and went on up to the scales with them anyway. I was desperately in need of a cold drink of water. It was not hard to see that if I was going to make any real money, as the girls promised me that I could, with doing this picking-cotton job, I was going to have to get better at it.

Daddy usually got home later than I did because he had to unhitch the equipment and take the tractor to the shed. Grandma was cautiously sympathetic with me concerning the worm sting. She hated to see my pain but said it was important for me to toughen up. It was my first cotton worm, but it undoubtedly would not be my last.

She had never seen or heard of this Obe fellow either. She wasn't surprised he knew who we were. Daddy got around and he had a lot of friends that neither she nor I knew. Talking to someone about a dog was something Daddy did often. He liked his coon dogs best, next to me and his bottle of whiskey.

The following few mornings were only repetitions of the days prior, without the stinging worm incident. I worked harder every day to get better at picking cotton. I discovered there was a rhythm to it. Pick, pick, stuff in the sack, step, step, drag, pick, pick, stuff again, shake, shake, drag. Then it started all over again.

Leave it to me to find music where it normally couldn't be found. The faster the song in my head, the faster my hands flew, and the faster the cotton got crammed into my sack.

It was about an hour after dinner. I had been able to

accumulate only one hundred pounds that morning so far. If I pushed it, I could bring my total to one hundred and seventy-five pounds for the day. It was harder to make your weight in the afternoon after the dew was gone. That was why the morning weight was so important.

I had to push myself harder to do better than that! My pay would be five dollars and seventy-five cents for the entire day for one hundred and seventy five pounds of cotton. I made six dollars per day chopping. I had to bring my totals up. That was all there was to it. If the other girls could do it, so could I. Tomorrow I would try to get at least one hundred and fifty pounds before dinner. My goal was two hundred and fifty pounds per day. That would bring a total payment of seven dollars and fifty cents for the day.

There was no telling how long I had my head down plotting that strategy before coming up for air. I looked around for another whirlwind, but there was not one in sight.

Unfortunately, I was about to experience a different kind of whirlwind. Pushing my hands into my back to help straighten out the kinks, I was eventually able to stand upright.

I hoped to catch a breeze by throwing back my bonnet. That was when I saw the flashing lights coming from the other field. My dad was being handcuffed and led from the field by none other than Officer Oller.

Tossing off my strap, I quickly ran down the row. Hot tears fell down my panic-stricken face for the second time that week. Daddy saw me running toward them; so he asked Officer Oller to wait until I got there for him to explain.

"DADDY, WHAT'S HAPPENING?" I was so frightened and out of breath I could barely speak.

"They just want to take me in for questioning, Baby. It'll be all right. Don't worry. I didn't do anything wrong." If he was worried, he didn't show any signs of it.

"Here are the car keys, have Simp drive my car home if he will. I'll try to get there as soon as I can." Neither of us had noticed Mr. Bertram's arrival until he made his loud protest.

"Hey, Clete, where you going with my tractor driver?" he questioned.

"I was told to pick him up and bring him in, Asa. I'm just doing my job." Officer Oller almost sounded apologetic.

"He didn't do it, Clete."

"How do you know, Asa?" Officer Oller stopped and slowly turned around.

"I just do." Mr. Bertram insisted.

Daddy nodded to Mr. Bertram, then quietly got into the police car. He gave me another smile and wink of assurance and told me again not to worry.

Before heading back to the field, Mr. Bertram and I

watched as the car disappeared into the haze. I tucked the car keys into my jeans' pocket and scanned the field for Mr. Simpson.

I was wondering, why did they wait until now to take Daddy to jail if they had something against him all along? Did my father actually have a hand in that catastrophe? How would Grandma take this news?

Chapter Seventeen

Grandma's Little Lamb

GRANDMA WAS STANDING at her cook stove in the kitchen with her back to the door. Expecting to see Daddy, she was surprised to see me come in with Simp. "Where is Larson?" she questioned, as she noticed Daddy's empty car in the yard.

"Mrs. Strom, don't worry, but Clete Oller took Larson down to the jail for questioning. We're guessing it is more about Nate McDougal. Anyways, I drove his car and brought Meryl home." Simp tried to break the news to her as calmly as possible, but there was no way he or I could hide the concern found on our faces.

"Kat and me will come over after supper and see if you've heard anything." Simp laid the keys down on the table and left to tell Katty what was going on.

Grandma took the skillet off the stove and wilted into the chair at the end of the table. She was visibly shaken by this news. I also found a chair and we sat in silence, our minds racing and our hearts pounding within our chests.

I finally broke the silence and told her about how

Mr. Bertram spoke up for Daddy and assured Mr. Oller that Daddy didn't do anything.

"Larson has always had a drinking problem. He has never been able to control his temper, and it seems he always finds the worst people, to be around. I've tried and I've tried with him, but he has stubbornly gone his own way and done what he wanted to do, despite anything I said. How do you make someone want to do right?"

My heart hurt for her as she was once again taking my dad's actions upon herself. He was in trouble, not because she didn't teach him any better. He was in trouble because of the strong will he had all of my life, and she'd just confirmed that he'd had it all of his life also.

Grandma constantly tried to keep Daddy out of trouble and worried about him all the time. Today, she said she was upset because he continued to search out what she referred to as the "bad apples in the barrel". I had other words for them. They were nothing but no-goods that didn't care about rising to the top of the barrel. As hard as it was to admit to myself, Daddy was content to be right there in the barrel bottom with them. I thought that Ode guy was probably one of those rotten apples too, even if he had come to my rescue when I encountered the stinging worm.

"I don't know why my little lamb keeps on wanting to go play in the pig pen," Grandma continued sadly.

"Your little lamb…Daddy," I asked? He seemed like anything but a little lamb to me. I couldn't think of many other people who would use that term to define him either.

"Yes, I raised all of my boys to be upstanding, good people, and Larson has been nothing but a worry to me since he was big enough to get in trouble. I keep trying to pull him away from 'life's pig pens,' and he lets himself be drawn back to them every chance he gets. I have told him over and over again that he can't play in the pig pen and not come out smelling like a PIG"! The desperation was evident in her voice as it took on an upscale pitch.

It was obvious to me that the blindfolds of love caused her to be the only one who saw a 'little lamb,' when she looked at Daddy. Those with 20/20 vision could see he was nothing but a pig like the others in the pen. That realization about my own father again saddened me.

Just then, we heard the crunching of gravel from an approaching car. Mr. Bertram and Daddy strolled into the kitchen with a somewhat victorious, yet cautious look on their faces. Mr. Bertram had put up Daddy's bond so he was freed from jail, at least while the investigation continued.

Grandma and I, tears streaming down our faces, ran to him and hugged him tightly as if the gravitational tug of crime could have pulled him away from us again. Mr. Bertram mumbled something about Emmy would be looking down the road for him, then made a hasty exit. The sound of crunching gravel could be heard again as the three of us quietly sat down at the kitchen table.

"Mom," Daddy began, "I didn't kill Nate McDougal. I just want you to know that. I want you to know it too, Meryl Jean." I was not sure I had ever heard that tone of sincerity in my dad's voice before. For what it was worth, I couldn't help but believe him that time. Grandma told him she believed him also.

The three of us were startled by again hearing footsteps upon the porch. We were relieved to see it was the trio from next door. They had seen Mr. Bertram bring Daddy home and came over to see what happened.

"Simp, Katty, I want you all to know too that I had nothing to do with Nate's murder," Daddy repeated his plea once more, that time to them.

"We never thought you did, Lars," said Katty, who seemed to understand Daddy beyond his flaws. Her voice reached a level of comfort and softness as much as Katty's naturally thunderous voice could.

"I overheard some things that Ode feller was saying out in the field; and to tell you the truth, I think he knows more than he is a tellin', even if it might have been whiskey talking sometimes, instead of him. I was thinking Asa was going to order him to go on home and sleep it off at any minute, but he didn't. Out there in the field and the hot sun is no place to be full of whiskey; Lars, you know that for a fact," Simp added. Then he asked, "How do you know that feller, Lars?"

"Why....I met him at the auction in Doodlum Switch one night," daddy said. "The next thing I knew he was working for Asa. I think he's an all right guy. He's just a little rough lookin. I don't think he's a bad person, might drink a little too much but is probably harmless. Why, he even put tobacco juice on Meryl's stinging worm today," he justified.

I remembered Daddy told me he'd met Obe when they'd talked about a coon dog. Now he was down-playing his and Obe's connection to Simp, as though it was just a casual tip-of-the-hat at the auction. That made me suspicious about just how my dad really knew that man. Obe and Daddy seemed quite familiar with one another while in the field. I remembered again the crooked smile and salute he gave Daddy as he walked back to his sack and mumbled something about wrong places and wrong times. There was suspicion with the story of how he and Daddy knew each other, but I wasn't sure what it was.

"Why did Clete feel like he had anything to question you any more about?" Simp inquired.

"Oh, that detective didn't like the size of my shoes, it seems. That was what he was bending down taking a picture of on the ground, that day he left here. It was my shoe print. Like I am the only one in these parts that has big, man-size feet," Daddy laughed.

Simp turned a little red with that remark. He had always taken a lot of teasing about having such small feet for a man. He wouldn't have anything to worry about, if the size of his feet had been the ones in question. They decided to call it a night. Sadie was amazingly quiet through all of this, but it was close to her bed-time and she just might have been sleepy. It occurred to me again how cruel people could be. With

Simp's case, it was about something too small, in contrast to how I had been teased about being too large. I guess Polly was right: if people wanted to torment you, they would find something to do it about.

We had a very late supper that night. Grandma cleaned up the kitchen and I went about getting my sponge bath. Daddy said he needed to go and get some gas for his car. He still wasn't back when Grandma and I gave it up and went on to bed. I was so tired, it didn't take me long to fall asleep. I figured that Grandma slept with one eye open until her 'little lamb's' return.

Chapter Eighteen

Unweaving a Tangled Web

GRANDMA HAD WANTED to go see Minnie McDougal since first hearing about her run-in with Nate. Soon after Minnie came home from the hospital, Grandma paid her a visit. I was asked to tag along to help carry food and rose-cuttings. Grandma never paid an empty-handed visit to anyone. The early morning rain had left too much water in the middles to work in the field anyways, so I agreed. After all, the concern of running into Nate was over. He was dead. We were, however, about to run into another whirlwind experience awaiting us down our path that would affect Minnie and us together—yet separately.

The McDougals lived a considerable distance back off the gravel road, on the edge of Number Eight Ditch. Each of us carried a rose cutting in one hand and I, a basket of fried chicken and Grandma a fresh peach cobbler in the other. We carefully negotiated the unkempt dirt path leading to Minnie's house, while also watching for snakes and poisonous weeds. The sweet smell of wild honeysuckle filled the air. Poison ivy and poison sumac vines mingled so evenly with the honeysuckle that edged the path, it was as though they had purposely been planted there. Grandma always said nature and life were a lot alike. The bad usually had its way of trying to wrap around the good.

It was quite a walk for a sixty-seven year old woman. But, an active lifestyle and hard work had left Grandma in good shape for someone her age; nevertheless, she became winded.

While stopping for her to catch her breath, we heard loud voices coming from the other side of the under-brush. Curious, we peeked through the barrier to investigate. This was when the first winds of our approaching whirlwind began to blow.

A usually soft-spoken Asa Bertram and another man were in a heated argument. There was no doubt he was upset with this man.

Prancing back and forth in desperation, Asa exclaimed, "You know and I know what happened to Nate."

"It was an accident, Asa, you saw it all," the stranger shouted back while holding his head in his hands.

"Yes, it was an accident. That's all the more reason you aint gonna' let Lars Strom take the blame for this. If he hadn't helped you clean up your still, that big-nosed detective would've found it and you'd be in jail for moonshinin'. You have to tell them what happened. You saved that poor woman's life. If you hadn't got that monster off her when you did, he would've killed her for sure. I saw that with my own eyes. I was about to help her myself before I saw you running over to them."

"Asa, you know how it is when you done time, the law aint gonna believe anythin' I tell em'. When they find out how we know each other and our your past, they aint gonna believe you either."

"Listen, Obe, my wife and daughter knows I done time. Lars Strom knows I done time too. It's just the other so-called good people in this town that might not be so understandin' if they knew it. You know what? How they see it is not important to me anymore."

"Well, what are we gonna do?"

"I'll get with Lars, and we'll figure it out and get back with you. Until we do, you need to just go on as usual. If you disappear, they'll surely suspect you. Maybe Lars can help figure a way out of this for all of us. He's figured himself out of enough things in the past. Come on, I'll take you to the field, we can tell them I picked you up and gave you a ride."

Asa, shaking his head as they left showed he was having trouble believing his own solution to the situation, but it was all they had to work with at that time.

As soon as the men were out of sight, Grandma and I worked our way on down the path to the McDougal house. We were shocked with what we had just overheard! The biggest shock being that Asa Bertram had been in prison! The next that Daddy had known about it! Grandma no longer doubted everything that I had said about that old codger Obe. She confirmed that he was about the dirtiest man she had ever seen!

MINNIE MCDOUGAL WAS sitting in her rocking chair on the porch, as though she was lost in a fog. Minnie didn't acknowledge our arrival at first.

SITTING WITHOUT SAYING a word, Grandma gently placed her hand over Minnie's. I took the food to the kitchen and filled an empty coffee can with water to keep the cuttings fresh until they could be planted. I quietly joined them back on the porch.

After a while, Minnie began to slowly speak. "Nate is gone, Alice."

"I know, Minnie, I am so sorry," Grandma heard and sympathized with Minnie's pain. A mother's love was constant, despite what her child did or said. I knew Grandma knew that first-hand.

"Alice, I feel like my very heart has been ripped out of me and I am left open to heal on my own. I know Nate didn't do right, but I loved him. He was my son." Minnie began to cry and slipped back into her malaise.

After a moment, Minnie continued. "That man didn't mean for Nate to die. He was only trying to keep him from hurting me any more than he already had."

"What man, Minnie?" I scooted closer to the edge of my chair but kept silent.

"I don't know who he was. I only know his name is Obe, because that's what I heard someone from behind the bushes calling him. He pulled Nate off of me. Then Nate slipped and hit his neck on a stump and fell into the ditch. I must have passed out because the next thing I knew, I was laying here on the porch. I guess I fainted again because when I came to myself, I was in the hospital." Minnie was doing her best at trying to put all the pieces together.

"Minnie, why were you wandering down around that ditch so late at night?"

"I heard that Nate had escaped jail. I figured he'd be hidden out down there in Asa Bertram's deer stand. He'd go there often to throw rocks in the water and talk to his father.

Grandma was confused. Any mention of Nate's father had always been obscure. "His father, I didn't think Nate ever knew his father. Wasn't Zed killed before Nate was born?"

"He was, but I tried to keep Nate's father's memory alive in his mind. I think it made him feel better to have talks with Zed."

"Minnie, did he ever talk about things to you too?"

"Nate didn't like my answers; so he didn't say much to me about the things he would talk to Zed about."

"How do you know what he talked to him about?"

"I went down to the ditch one evening to call Nate in for supper. He was up in Asa's deer stand as usual. I could hear him talking to someone. I listened for another voice, but the only voice to be heard was Nate's.

Alice, he was crying, asking Zed to tell him why he was different and why he did the things he did. Nate knew people hated him. He kept telling his daddy how sorry and ashamed he was. He asked Zed to help him do better.

Of course, he could make up whatever answers he wanted to hear from Zed. I assume his imagination gave him the answers he wanted since he was smiling when he came down. It startled him to see me there; but I never let him know I overheard. I was encouraged after hearing Nate admit that he knew he was doing wrong. If a person knows they do wrong, then maybe they can change. Do you believe that, Alice?"

"Yes, Minnie, I do. The only way a body can fix what's wrong with them is to first find out what's not right. It's so sad to think that poor boy thought the only person he could talk to that would understand him, was his dead father. If it helped him to talk to his daddy, then it was good for him to do it." Grandma later confessed that possibly—she along with many others— could have been a little more charitable toward Nate McDougal while they'd had the chance.

"MINNIE, WHY DID he always go to the deer stand to

talk to his father?" Grandma wondered why it was any different from any other place he could go and talk to his dad.

"I used to tell Nate a lot of Bible stories. I told him how Moses would go up on the mountain to talk to God and how God spoke to him in a burning bush. The deer stand was a high place; so I'm guessing Nate thought it was like Moses' mountain.

He thought he heard voices in the water rushing over the rocks in the ditch which was like God talking from a bush.

Nate was simple Alice, but he had a big imagination. The deer stand was Nate's mountain. As far as I know, it was the only place that Nate went to talk to Zed, so that is where I went to look for him that night. I'm thinking that was why Nate escaped jail, so he could go talk to his Daddy in the only place he thought he could find him.

When I found Nate, I tried to warn him that the law was lookin' for him. I tried to get him to turn himself in. He wouldn't listen. He got mad and started roughin' me up again. The next thing I remember, before I fainted, was this man yelling Nate's name and telling him to stop.

My mind must have been playing tricks on me too. Alice, it sounded just like Zed! Anyway, this person knew Nate somehow because he kept calling his name. Then, I heard someone yellin' 'Obe, Obe,' from behind the bushes is the only reason I know this man's name." Minnie's brow wrinkled as she struggled to remember.

"So actually, this Obe fellow saved your life. Nate really wasn't murdered. He fell and broke his neck when he heard Obe yelling to him. Is that right?" Grandma was pressing Minnie for the answer she herself needed to hear.

Minnie nodded in agreement and started to slip away again.

"Minnie, I know it is going to be painful for you, but you must tell Clete Oller this story. They need to know that Nate was not murdered. They are frantically trying to find someone to blame for his death. Can you, will you, be willing to do that? I'll go with you if you want me there."

Minnie agreed to go give Clete Oller her account of what happened to Nate.

"Yes, I'll go tell 'em. I don't want someone to hafta' take the blame for somethin' they didn't do. Yes, I'd like it if you'd go with me, Alice."

"I'll be right beside you when you tell them, Minnie. Would you want me to ask my son Larson to take us to Mr. Oller's office in his car?" Grandma admitted later of how glad she was to get that mystery cleared up for lots of reasons, her own son's innocence being one of them. The town's folk needed to know there wasn't a murderer on the loose. Most of all, she hoped that for Minnie to get it out in the open might have helped her dear friend to begin the healing process.

I made coffee. Grandma coaxed Minnie into eating a little of the cobbler before getting her to lie down, until we could return with Daddy.

Arriving at the cotton patch, we found Daddy up to his chin in tractor grease. Asa was standing along side and watching. No one could help Daddy with any of his mechanic jobs. He didn't work well with others. He said they asked too many questions and got in the way. He allowed Asa to stand by and possibly hand him a wrench from time to time, as long as he would move over when he was told to do so, and kept quiet. Asa and Daddy left the tractor standing in the field as soon as we shared our information with them. Asa stopped to alert his wife, with a promise of telling her more later on. Then he and Obe rushed to prepare Clete for what was about to happen.

Daddy drove us as far as the narrow dirt path would allow. After whipping the car around and backing it up for a quick getaway, he, Grandma and I took the rest of the path on foot to get Minnie.

A cloud of dust was all that remained as Daddy pointed his car toward Clete Oller's office with Grandma, me, and Minnie inside.

DETECTIVE DESMOND STROLLED through the door shortly after we arrived. Clete offered him a chair and advised him to get his notebook ready. Asa had already taken his position at the end of the table. Obe found himself a place near the corner of the room, several feet away from the others. He was leaned back in a cane-bottom chair and as was his custom, his head was down, and his eyes were focused on the floor, only looking up occasionally.

Daddy and the two ladies had chairs already waiting for them. They weren't expecting me, but after Daddy assured them I could stay, I was also provided a chair and the meeting began.

THOUGH SHE HAD difficulty, Minnie McDougal quietly recalled the entire incident just as she remembered it: "I knew the law'd be lookin' for Nate since he'd escaped jail. I guessed that he'd be hiding out at Mr. Bertram's deer stand. He'd go there and sit a lot. Soon as I saw him, I called him down and started beggin' him to turn himself in, knowin' they'd find him sooner or later. We argued. He tried to run, but I held on to his sleeve. He jerked away, then turned on me. He was yellin' and I was screamin'. He slapped me, hit my nose and blood went everywhere. I heard someone shoutin', "Nate, let her go."

When Nate heard his name, he turned around real fast to see who was yellin' at him. That was when his foot slipped on a flat rock near the bank of the ditch. He fell. His head and neck hit a big piece of driftwood that washed up on the bank. I could tell his neck was broke from how he was layin'. He was half in the mud and half in the water and he wasn't movin' at all. I don't know what happened next. I guess I fainted."

Minnie took a deep breath to regain her composure and began again with her account.

"Later, I was layin' on my front porch and your deputy was leaned over me and askin' if I was ok, Mr. Oller. He said he came a lookin' for Nate but found me instead all sprawled out on my porch in a muddy, bloody mess with a coat doubled up under my head. I didn't know how I or the coat got there. They found my Nate, floatin' in the ditch," Minnie cried as she once more relived the memory of her dead son.

"I couldn't talk about it till Alice Strom came over to see me. Alice, you're a good friend. Your voice was as kind and sweet as an angel talkin' to me.

I know if there's anyone who understands about lovin' a son that don't do right, it is you, Alice." Minnie obviously had forgotten about Daddy sitting in the room.

I figured Daddy probably wasn't bothered by Minnie's perceptions. He was used to hearing people's first and second hand opinions of him. Daddy was thick-skinned in that way.

"Mr. Oller, Alice said y'all are lookin' real hard to find the one who killed Nate. I'm here to tell you that NO ONE KILLED NATE! I saw him fall. I saw my boy's neck all broke and twisted when he was layin' there in the mud and water! NO ONE KILLED NATE, it was an accident! He fell on his own accord!"

Minnie's cry was so heart-wrenching. It was difficult for even tough, rough Daddy and gruff, old Obe, along with the others in the room, to hold back the tears.

Asa Bertram confirmed Minnie's story. He said he was headed to his deer stand when he heard a ruckus over near the bend of the ditch. He saw and heard the argument and saw Nate slip, fall, and break his neck.

What Asa added was what he witnessed while Minnie was unconscious. "Obe ran toward the battling pair, gathered Minnie McDougal up in his arms and carried her off. He took her to her porch and put his coat under her head."

That was the first time Minnie McDougal noticed the dirty person sitting over in the corner of the room.

"Thank you, sir. Your name is Obe? Thank you for keepin' Nate from hurtin' me that night and gettin' me to my porch. I know you didn't cause Nate to die. You were only trying to keep him from hurting me any more," she said in her quiet, awkward way.

Obe grunted out a "you're welcome, M'am," barely taking his eyes away from the floor.

Chapter Nineteen

A Revealing Meeting at Clete's Office

THERE HAD BEEN no mention of Obe's still. Due to Daddy's help and quick thinking, the evidence was gone; long before the authorities came snooping around.

Asa's being there was never questioned, since going hunting wasn't a crime. Also my dad was right; there were other people around who had feet as big as his. It just so happened Obe's feet were the same size as Daddy's. It was only natural that his big footprints were all along the ditch bank since he'd been living in a shack nearby.

Daddy's footprints were there because he admitted going to talk to Obe about a dog. His passion for dogs, and hunting was common knowledge to almost everyone, so that didn't seem at all out of the ordinary.

Now, there was this nagging question as to why Obe, Daddy or Asa Bertram never came forward with the evidence about Nate, since the three of them witnessed the whole thing.

Asa whispered to Clete and told him they would be glad to clear up that part of it after the two ladies and the little girl had left the room. Clete suggested that Grandma and I take Minnie into the outer office for some fresh air and water.

DADDY DIDN'T SHARE with us right away about what was said in that closed-door meeting. He revealed 'bits and pieces' of certain details eventually, when he thought it was time for us to know them, but I never confessed that I had heard most of it first hand. It wasn't my intention to eavesdrop. It was totally accidental.

Grandma had left her purse in Mr. Oller's office and asked me to go get it for her before the meeting resumed. I quietly cracked the door but before I could ask for Grandma's purse, the mention of my dad's name from Obe's solemn voice stopped me abruptly. Obe, hadn't anything to say until that time, but had now decided to join into the conversation.

"Lars and Asa didn't say anythin' because they were coverin' for me," Obe said boldly.

So daddy knew something all along as Grandma and I had feared.

"I don't understand. All they had to do was come forth, say they saw it and it wouldn't have been a problem. Then, I wouldn't have spent all this time trying to pin it on Larson Strom here or his mother's neighbors," Detective Desmond complained.

"Well, they knew my past. They knew I was in prison for a while. If that'd got out, y'all woulda' quit lookin' for anyone else and locked me up from the start, Sheriff, and you know it," he reasoned as he directed his statement to Clete.

Just as Grandma said, daddy knew a lot of people that we didn't know. However, it was shocking to hear he was pals with and even went to the extent of covering up for someone who had been in prison.

While Clete was trying to decide if Obe had just made an accurate assumption or if he could defend that accusation in any way, Asa chimed in.

"Alright, Clete, I'll own up to it. I was in prison with Obe here. That was how I knew him," Asa confessed.

My feet became riveted to the floor, upon hearing Asa Bertram's risky confession to Clete Oller and Detective Desmond concerning his prison stay.

Clete's reaction to Asa's confession seemed to be one of relief and irritation in equal measures.

"Do you really think you are telling me something I don't already know, Asa? What kind a law man do you think I am? I've known this for most of my life. I also know you didn't deserve to be there. More people than you can guess have always known that Carl Chaffin, not you, pulled the trigger that night in the dance hall and killed the man who was ruffin' up his sister, and you took the sentence that belonged to him."

Mr. Chaffin shot someone! I knew these confessions were not meant for my ears, but I was in too deep to turn away by then.

"Man, I'm glad to get that off my chest," Clete Oller said with a sigh of relief. Although that dance hall incident happened when I was still just a kid, the story had been passed down many times. I know it also happened, Asa, before you and Emerald got married. She and Carl Chaffin's sister were friends, right? Not only did she know the story; she was there in the hall, the night it all happened. Gossip found some of the town's folk questioning why a squeaky clean person such as Emerald would agree to marry a man who had been in prison."

"Well, Emmy was never one who leaned heavily on other people's assumptions or opinions, so she paid little attention to their comments," Asa explained.

"Carl promised me a good parcel of farm land after I got out of prison, if I'd take the blame and serve the sentence in his place. There aint many people who trust a business man with a prison record," Asa added.

"I thought about it for a long time, but finally agreed. Chaffin kept his promise and hired one of the best lawyers in the country to get my time cut short, since the whole ordeal was in defense of his sister. He also somehow pulled some strings and kept himself clear of the sticky mess.

That's how Emmy and me got our cotton farm. Nobody in my family ever had any money to speak of. We had a lot of ambition but not much education. I knew it was a chance for us to have the dream we probably could have never had on our own." It was as though Asa was finding peace in his decision for losing his own reputation to gain his cotton farm.

While everyone was silently considering Asa's past decisions, Obe broke the silence in the room and continued, "Jobs don't come around easy for me, so I came to Asa here for work."

"What were you in prison for?" Desmond demanded of Obe.

"Suspicion of robbery," he admitted.

"Suspicion, did you do it or not?" Desmond asked with a smirk.

"No...I didn't do it. I was sleepin' in a box car that night. Zed McDougal ran up on me and I thought he mighta' come to start trouble. See, she don't remember me cause' it was many years ago. I let myself run down a lot, but I knew Minnie McDougal before she and Zed got hitched,"

"Just how would you know Minnie McDougal? It sure don't look like you two would have been running in the same circles," Desmond's question dripped with sarcasm.

"Well, we did," an obviously annoyed Obe, spouted back. "Like I said," he resumed. "I let myself run down a lot. Minnie and I have a past. We'd planned to be married. I decided I needed to go off and find better work somewhere. Y'all know if you don't have a farm or a business of some kind or you're a lawman in these parts; there ain't much of a livin' to be made around here other than pickin' and choppin' cotton." That remark was directed to Clete Oller.

"I got this job near St. Louis buildin' barges. I guess Minnie thought I was gone for good 'cause I never made any contact with her for almost two months. She probably thought I got cold feet and ran but I didn't. By the time I got back, she'd married Zed McDougal.

I looked her up as soon as I could, but she told me she'd already married Zed, thinkin' I was never comin' back. Minnie said she loved me and not Zed. She was goin' to tell him the whole story and maybe he'd let her out of the marriage. I reckoned she'd told him and he was mad and comin' after me since he was comin alone."

"Well, that wouldn't land you in prison. If just two men arguing over a woman is all it was," said Desmond.

"I found out later I just thought that Zed was there at the track lookin' for me. We only both happened to be at the same place at the wrong time."

He glanced over to get Daddy's reaction since that was the example they used out in the cotton patch that day.

"Zed never saw me. He didn't know I was sleepin' there in a boxcar. He came to meet some other fellers who had robbed a chicken fightin' gang. They'd let Zed hold the money for em' til things quieted down with the promise of givin' him a cut of the wad. He'd never been in trouble before, but maybe he thought it'd be a quick and easy way to rake up a little extra cash. Who knows?

Zed started to hand em' the money, and that's when

they drew a gun on him. He tossed the wad up into the box car where I was hidin' before they could take it from him. He pulled his gun from the inside pocket of his coat and fought with 'em. He and one of 'em got shot amongst' all the gunfire, and the other feller ran off. Zed didn't know it, but the law was onto 'em and followin' 'em. They wern't followin' close enough though. They didn't make it there before Zed and one of the robbers died.

They found me and the money in the box car and thought I was the third robber. I couldn't prove I wasn't 'cause all the witnesses had been shot and the real robber ran off. I was in prison for three years when the real robber got caught red-handed tryin' to steal again. He got tricked into confessin' to the first robbery that I was thrown in prison for, so I was let go. Asa and I were in prison together at the same time, and both of us were innocent of what we were in there for."

Still listening and afraid to breathe for fear of being discovered, like a statue, I stayed put.

"Well, I got a couple of questions. For one thing, why did Minnie marry Zed so fast if it was you she really wanted? Another thing, after Zed was dead, then why didn't you and Minnie just go on and marry then?" By that time, Clete's questions were more about Obe and Minnie's love story than about Nate McDougal's death, which was supposed to be the real reason for their meeting.

"When I came back from St. Louis to tell Minnie about my new job and all, before she told me about her and Zed marrin', she told me an even more surprisin' sumthin'. She was havin' a baby. That's why she married Zed so fast."

The room was silent as everyone's mouth had dropped open in astonishment.

"Look, I know you been writin' this all down, but I'm hopin' that none of this don't have to be told outside of this room detective," Obe requested of Detective Desmond.

"Not unless it links you to some other crime. I don't see it having anything to do with the Nate McDougal incident so far," said Desmond.

"Well, I guess you can say the only crime was Minnie and me were two young kids and thought we loved each other. Zed did what he thought was the right thing for protecting Minnie. The good ladies of the town had a habit of checkin' their calendars real close when babies come so soon after a weddin'. I guess I couldn't blame Zed for bein' mad at me, especially if Minnie told him it was me who she loved and not him. Of course, like I said, I guess he wasn't lookin' for me. He was tryin' to meet up with those robber fellers."

"I have to ask again," Clete pursued his original question. "Why didn't you and Minnie just get married and go on from there?" It seemed like a simple solution to Clete after all he'd heard.

"She was havin' a baby. Everyone looked at her as a poor widow whose unborn baby's father had just got innocently killed. I didn't wanta bring more shame on her than I already had. I was on my way to prison even if it was for sumthin' I didn't do. I thought it was better for the baby to grow up being told his daddy was accidentally shot than…his daddy was a ex con."

"But it was his daddy that got shot…his daddy wasn't the ex…"

Obe interrupted Detective Desmond. "No, his daddy was the ex con. I was Nate's real daddy," Obe sighed as he confessed to being Nate's father. "I decided it was best to leave things the way they was. People didn't want to hire me. I thought Minnie would meet and marry someone good and give 'em a better life, but now I find out she never did."

Asa Bertram almost fell off his stool. "Well, I never, we shared prison cells and innocence for three years, but this is the first time you ever shared that bit of information with me or I'm guessing, anyone else.

"I don't get it: why didn't Minnie McDougal recognize you just now?" Clete interjected his fourth question.

"I was shackin' up there around the bend on the ditch bank so that ever once in a while, I could get a glimpse of Minnie and Nate. I don't think Minnie ever knew I was livin' there. Nate would see me from time to time, but he just thought I was hoboin' and really never paid me much mind. I hated how Nate turned out, but I didn't see there was any fixin' him; so I had to just let it go. After all, he was grown. Aint no way I can 'lick that calf over again,' after the damage is done. Y'all hafta' know I wouldn't a harmed my own flesh and blood. He fell on that stump too quick for me to do anythin'. I was only tryin' to get his attention turned away from Minnie before he hurt her bad. Minnie didn't see me that night. She was already passed out. The least I could do was get her out of the mud and away from Nate's dead body laying there in the ditch," Obe explained. "Anyways, I don't think my own mother would recognize me lookin' like this, all shabby and dirty and my hair long and gray."

"Didn't she at least pick up on anything when she kept hearing people calling you Obe," inquired Clete.

"No, she never knew me as Obe. That is the nickname I picked up while I was in the pen. Obe is short for Obadiah. I come up with the Stone part. My real last name is…McDougal. Zedekiah McDougal was my brother.

The silence in the room at that point was deadening. The other four people in that room could not believe what they had just heard. Neither could I.

"McDougal!" Asa exclaimed.

"If that don't beat anything I ever heard," Daddy said in disbelief and slapped his hat against his leg. "All the time that Asa and me have known you, we didn't even know your real last name?" He was almost embarrassed that he hadn't put all of that together. I think Daddy gave himself more than his share of credit for being knowledgeable about the *real world* since he had always considered himself as being such a big part of it.

"So let me get this straight. You're Nate's real dad, and you're Zed McDougal's own brother. Got any more surprises for us?" Asa sounded almost betrayed.

"Well, maybe."

"What else could there be to top that?" Daddy, who had stood up, sat back down to hear what was next.

"Zed and me had another brother. We were all born at the same time."

"You mean you were triplets?" Clete clarified.

"Aw, no…," moans Asa.

"So you're saying there were two others like you? Aw, no…not three Obes?" Daddy laughingly asked.

"Well, Zed is dead, where's the other brother and what's his name?" Detective Desmond wanted to know.

"He died being born. His name was Malachi; seemed my mother liked Bible names."

"Well, you did it. You topped it all. Are you done now?" Asa was stunned.

"I may be able to come up with somethin' later on, but guess that's enough for right now," Obe said teasingly.

Detective Desmond shut his book, slapped it with his hand, and announced to the room that as far as he was concerned the case was settled. There were four witnesses that could testify that Nate's death was an accident. He'd give them his report when he got back to Springfield, and they could do what they wanted with it. As far as he could see, his job was done!

"You all have made a fool out of me, wasted my time, and a lot of taxpayer's good money when all you needed to do was come forth in the first place. I'm done with the whole crazy lot of you! All I want to do now is to get out of this mud-bogged, clod-hopping little town, get back to Springfield and work on some real cases! Sheriff Oller, you'll be getting a copy of my report when it is completed," and slammed the door on his way out. He almost ran over me as he left but didn't seem to realize or care that I had heard the entire conversation of their meeting.

Clete waited until he heard Desmond's car take off, then began. "Well…he can write and send all the reports he wants to. That may be how they do it in Springfield, but we have our own way of doing things around here.

Obe, you did a good thing by saving Minnie McDougal's life. Asa, you and Lars might could have handled it a little differently, but after hearing all the story, I guess I understand why you did what you did. Now all of you stay put for a while and keep your noses clean till this clears up. I want to caution each one of you to be careful who and what you tell about what went on in this meeting this afternoon. Now, don't all three of y'all have a cotton field to tend to?" Clete also slammed his book down as Detective Desmond did and glared at them until they cleared his office and shut the door behind them.

Daddy saw me once he reached the door and I asked him to get Grandma's purse. As far as he knew, I had just stepped inside the room.

DADDY AND OBE went back to the field to finish out the day. Asa, Grandma and I took Minnie home, then Asa rushed back to the field. We stayed with Minnie long enough to see that she ate something, then took the path home to make our own supper.

One of the 'bits' of the meeting, Daddy chose to share with us during supper was that Detective Desmond officially declared Nate's death to be an accident and closed the book on his part of all of it. The big 'piece' of the details—the most shocking part—of Obe being Nate's father and Zed McDougal's brother was left out. He thought that private baggage of information was too heavy a load for us to carry around at that time. I never let him know that I had been eavesdropping at the door. It had been a long time since I had gotten a belt whipping but I feared he might think eavesdropping could be reason for one. I would tell Grandma though, when I got the chance.

Finally, we were all glad to call it a day and go to bed. I was more than relieved that most of all, my dad was no longer a suspect in a murder. The picture of Nate McDougal's muddy body lying in Number Eight Ditch continued to replay over and over in my mind. Surprisingly, I felt compassion for that hated man that I once had feared so much.

I also couldn't stop thinking about his poor mother. Would she be able to find peace about her son's death now that Detective Desmond had closed the case? I truly hoped so for Minnie's sake.

Unfortunately, the sleep that eventually overtook me

was again interrupted by my reoccurring dream of being stuck in the mud as I screamed for help. Waking, I kept reminding myself that I was not in the mud, but safe and sound in my own bed. Daddy and Grandma were peacefully sleeping in the next room. Why did that dream keep haunting me? I should have been sleeping soundly after the turn of the day's events. Sleep finally did come, and it was a good thing. After all, the cotton field would be calling me very early, come morning.

Chapter Twenty

Putting The Puzzle Together

SCARLETT WAS SICK; so only Tara and Melly were in the wagon that next morning when it stopped to let me board. Mr. Bertram had shared the entire private conversation from the day before with his wife, despite Obe's request that it not be told. Asa was confident that Emmy would take it to heart, and that it wouldn't end up as idle gossip. She knew most of it already; it was only right she knew the rest.

Emmy said that she was relieved there wasn't a murderer on the loose to threaten her little town. To hear that the same Obe that was working alongside us every day was Nate's father and Zed's brother was most shocking. It was hard to imagine that behind that hard, dirty exterior beat the heart of a man who had held such a tender love for Minnie all those years.

Yes, Emmy remembered a lot of calendars being checked after the hasty wedding between Minnie and Zed. However, that was overshadowed by Zed's untimely death. She had never heard any talk about Obe and Minnie. If that was ever big news, her sister Effie must have missed it.

The McCrady girls were also only told that Nate's death was an accident and that the case was closed. Although, I wanted to let them in on my eavesdropping secret more than anything, I didn't think it was wise to tell them just yet. I couldn't take a chance on Daddy finding out.

Everyone was glad Detective Desmond had gone back to Springfield, where they all felt he belonged. Not one member of the McCrady, Bertram, Strom, or Simpson families was sad to see him go! Miss Katty and Simp were at the top of that list. Miss Katty didn't have time for his big-city attitude for sure!

Tara's cheerleader friend, Carla was in our field that day since the first picking of her dad's patch was done. Cheerleaders might have been part of an elite group at school, but in the cotton field, everyone put on the strap of their sack the same way.

They paired up and started talking about cheer routines. Before long, Melly and I were at the head of the pack, and we were even picking grab rows. To pick grab rows, you picked your own row, plus shared a row in between you and the picker next to you. It helped to get your sack filled faster, and your totals added up more quickly. I was driven to reach my goal of a hundred and fifty pounds of cotton before noon. If for not having to fight off the giant blue-steel billed mosquitoes that lit on us biting, we might could have even worked more speedily.

If Grandma saw too many more bites on me, she

would carry out her threat to dose me with quinine and sugar. She said most people added it to their diet year round to fight malaria. I didn't think it possible that she could add enough sugar to mask the taste of the quinine to suit me. Melly said her Grandma Bertram saw that she and her sisters got dosed with it regularly.

Tara and Carla were talking faster than they were picking and soon lagged behind. After being on the receiving end of many tongue-lashings from her Grandmother in the past, I thought maybe Tara should have been more concerned.

Comfortably being beyond earshot of the rest, I shared my dream with Melly. She then took the opportunity to share that she too had a reoccurring dream. She dreamed of being chased by a huge gorilla. In each dream she ran from room to room within a tall, dark building and barely escaped his grasp and open mouth. She thought maybe her dream stemmed from seeing the movie "King Kong" when she was younger and it scared her almost to death!

I hadn't seen a lot of movies. In Brookstown, I was sometimes, but not often, allowed to go to a Sunday matinee. I tried to recall if I had ever seen a movie about mud or someone being stuck in it. If so, I couldn't remember. Melly wasn't much help.

Eventually, we heard Mrs. Bertram's shrill voice shrieking from mid-way of the field.

"Tara Gayle, you and Carla need to save your cheer-leading talk for places other than the cotton patch. Look how far y'all are behind Jean and Melly Ann. Your sacks don't have hardly any cotton in them at all. Now, get to pickin' that cotton!"

Melly and I were relieved that it was Tara and Carla, and not us, who were the objects of her Grandmother's wrath. Cotton soon started flying into their sacks. They were almost caught up when the dinner bell rang. We were all ready for that.

I passed by that Obe fellow on my way back to the patch after dinner. I saw him a little differently now since he was a hero for Minnie McDougal. Putting his coat under her head proved him to be more sensitive than anyone, including me, had given him credit.

Daddy tried to tell me Obe wasn't a bad person the day he rescued me from that worm. He said Obe just had a lot of life hanging on him. I thought that maybe it might have been a good thing if he washed a little of it off from time to time, but that was just me.

It was obvious Mr. Bertram needed a new tractor. The one he had now was down again, and Daddy was working late trying to fix it. Grandma had his supper waiting on the stove as usual. The kitchen chores done and my sponge bath over, I joined her on the swing to wait for him.

"It could be all your hard work in the field is helping you to slim down a bit. You may be even getting taller," she noted.

I hoped that to be true. Talking about my weight opened the door to a few questions I'd had for a long time.

"Grandma, why are all of my cousins thin, you

know, normal size and I'm overweight? I am the only fat one in the bunch." I usually avoided talking about weight. The word fat was hurtful to hear, even out of my own mouth, but our porch swing and Grandma's heart were *safe places*, so it was okay.

"Well, part of it is probably because your mother and your dad are not small people. You just got it naturally from them."

"Well, Miss Katty nor the McCrady girls' mother sure aren't small women, and neither of the girls or Sadie is big. Was I always fat?" I asked using that offensive word again.

"Oh no, you were just barely five pounds when you were born. Matter of a fact, we were worried about you for a while because you were so small. Your mother nursed you until it was discovered that she only had 'blue john.'"

"Blue john, what's that?"

"It's watery breast milk that is not rich enough to nourish babies as it should."

"Is it really blue?"

"It's got a bluish tinge to it, yes."

"Then how was it that I grew so fat?"

"The doctor advised your mother to feed you half water and half Pet Milk. Almost everybody fed their babies Pet Milk back then, if they didn't have rich breast milk. You still didn't grow. You'd suck that bottle 'till the veins in your neck would stick out! You pulled so hard you got a rupture and had to wear a special made truss for a while.

"I remember Mama and Daddy talking about that truss and about how small it was. Daddy bragged that he was the only one that could *fix* my rupture because Mama was too scared to try."

"Yes, I have seen your mom run out on their back porch waving her arms, and you'd be screaming your head off. Your dad would be working in the field next to their house. He'd hear y'all screaming and he'd jump off of his tractor and run all the way to get to you. He'd grab you by your feet, hold you up-side-down and rub that little rupture back in place. When you stopped crying, he would go back to work. Why he would've waded mud and high waters to get to you when that little thing would pooch out."

Grandma was always glad to brag on anything good that Daddy did.

"Well, then, why did I get fat anyway, if I couldn't suck the milk out of the bottle?" None of what she was telling me was adding up.

"Luckily for you, one day when you all were over visiting your Grandpa Omar and me, your Grandpa saw you struggling to suck your bottle and noticed the veins in your neck. He told me to give that bottle to him. He didn't think you were getting any milk out of it. Then, he sent me to fetch my big darning needle and a box of matches. He held the needle under a match until it got red hot then stuck it into the end of the nipple making a bigger hole. After that, your Mama gave you that bottle and you downed it in no time. You started gaining weight and doing better right away. Your rupture disappeared, and you no longer needed the truss."

She was proud to give her husband, my Grandpa Omar, the credit for discovering that I was almost starved to death and he solved the mystery.

"Grandpa Omar saved your life, Meryl, I do believe."

"Why didn't Mamma realize the hole wasn't big enough?"

"I don't know. Back then, almost everyone breast-fed their babies; only a handful of women bottle-fed them.

I had good rich milk when all of my babies were born. I never had to bottle-feed any of them and didn't know much about it. I was very little help to your Mama about that. Even though your mother was thirty-six years old when you were born, she hadn't had much experience in child-raising. She was only fourteen years old when your brother was born. Why, she was just a child herself."

Fourteen, to think, she became pregnant with my brother when she was only thirteen and turned fourteen seven months before he was born. Her birthday was in August and his was in March.

When Mama told me about having my brother at age fourteen, I was so young that fourteen was just a number. I couldn't have imagined getting pregnant at the age I was right then and having a baby at fourteen years old! My poor little mother.

"She wouldn't have known how to take care of your half brother at all, if it hadn't been for your Aunt Ercel."

Grandma continued.

"Really?"

"Yes, your mother's nineteen year old sister Ercel, was nursing her own baby at the time. She took turns nursing your brother and her baby too. It was even said she nursed them both at the same time, one on each breast. There must have not been anything wrong with her milk; that was a fact," she said on her way to the kitchen to get us some ice water.

I swung quietly and tried to absorb all of the new information she had just shared with me. So that was why I was such a fat baby and child. I knew Grandma saw my Grandpa as a hero, but I was not sure if I was happy with how he saved my life or mad at him for making the hole in the nipple bigger so I could be fed like a little "fattening-pig".

She brought our water and rejoined me in the swing. That tractor and mud picture was too familiar and lingered in my mind. I couldn't stop thinking about it.

"Grandma, do you recall a time when I was small that I got stuck in the mud and couldn't get out?"

I had never asked her about it before, but she seemed to be open to sharing things that night; so I thought that might have been a good time. She didn't seem anxious to answer; so I prodded her again.

"Can you remember me getting stuck in the mud, maybe when I was small? I often have this dream that I am stuck in the mud and I can see Daddy off across a field and I start screaming for him."

She took a deep breath, then began. "Okay, Meryl, I

was proud to tell you about your Grandpa fixing your bottle nipple and about how your dad fixed your rupture. I guess I'll have to tell you something I'm not real proud of, since you brought it up and feel like you have to know." She was speaking softly and choosing her words carefully.

Avoiding eye contact, her voice was somewhat broken as she began. "One spring day while your dad was plowing a field next to where you all lived, you somehow got out of your mother's sight long enough to go out on the back porch by yourself. You couldn't have been more than two, maybe two and a half years old. You were always so crazy about your Daddy."

Her solemn stare turned to a glowing smile as she once again found my father to be a source of pride.

"You saw him plowing out in the field and started making your way toward him. The spring rains had created a bog marsh between the house and the field where he was plowing.

You were too young to know not to go through the bog. You got stuck all the way up to your knees and couldn't get free. You know now, how gumbo can be when it gets wet. Your mother heard your screams. You were calling for your daddy, but he couldn't hear you over the noise of the tractor. As soon as Edna saw and heard you, she started running toward you. Your daddy finally looked up and saw all of the commotion. He stopped the tractor, jumped off, and also ran toward you.

The closer he got, the madder he became at the

thought of your mother not watching you closely enough. It also scared him to death that he could have accidentally run over you with the tractor without seeing you first.

He was outraged by the time he reached you and your mother. He…I am sorry to say, slapped Edna and she fell to her knees. Then he took off his belt and whipped you with it. He was so mad by that time he was completely out of control and wasn't thinking at all.

Between the combination of the heat, being scared and the whipping, I think you were crying so hard and holding your breath that you blacked out for a few minutes. It scared them both, when that happened, but everything had already been done. You came to yourself and seemed to be okay, as soon as your mother put a cold cloth on your face; so your Daddy went back to the field. She started washing the mud off of you and her both and held you on her lap until she saw you were going to be okay.

Meryl, I ran out on the porch and saw and heard it all, after hearing your screams, your mother's cries, and his cussing. I tried to calm him down and get him to stop, but he was just too mad. You know how your dad does when he gets that mad. Well…he wouldn't listen to me at all.

I know your dad was ashamed of what he had done. He was really sorry he slapped Edna and sorry for sure that he whipped you. His mind just wasn't working at all at that time, I really don't even think he knew what he was doing. I hoped that maybe he felt so badly about it all, that he would have never took his belt to you again. I don't think he did, for a long while after that.

I am sorry to say that was the way your Grandpa Omar punished our boys too. It was all your dad knew and how he thought it had to be done. I never saw you do anything to need a belt whipping for. You have always been such a *bitable* child."

Grandma used one of her favorite words for otherwise saying she thought I was always easy to discipline.

"It seemed to me that he could have just talked to you and got you to do what he wanted you to do.

I don't think he was even drinking that day at all. It was that awful 'Strom temper,' Meryl. It was that temper that I guess just got the best of him. That was one time that I almost wished his outburst could have been blamed on the bottle, but as far as I ever knew, it couldn't have been. I'm not proud to tell you about this, but since you asked, I guess it is my place to tell you now. You've never mentioned those dreams to me before. I didn't know you were having them."

We sat quietly for a while, after she related that story. I was the one to eventually break the silence.

"Grandma, I know you hated to tell me about that, but I'm glad you did. Thank you." It was as though my probing questions and her cutting words punctured her aged frame and deprived it of all strength and stamina. She slumped as she sat quietly beside me in the swing.

At first, I felt affected in much the same way. Then, surprisingly, I started to get an opposite reaction. A sense of strength mingled with peace flowed through me. I had found a missing puzzle piece and could now see the picture in its entirety. At last I knew where that dream was born and understood why I had such an obsession with mud.

"I hated to hear about Daddy hitting Mama and whipping me. Grandma, I've never told you this before but I've seen him hit her many times. You know about my whippings. I am hoping my whippings will be one of my 'nevers'. He for sure can never hit her again."

"Your 'nevers' Meryl, what do you mean your 'nevers?'"

"My 'nevers' are things I will *never* have to have in my life again. I hope never to have belt whippings again, never to have to wear boy shoes, and it is my plan *never* to allow people to make fun of me or torment me again for being fat. I know I am fat. I wish I wasn't. But that doesn't give anyone the right to torment or embarrass me and hurt my feelings because I am! I have more 'nevers' but those are the main ones for now."

As a woman who had devoted her life to her children and grandchildren, my list of 'nevers' broke Grandma's heart. If she hadn't realized it before, she knew now that she couldn't wrap her sons or me in a protective shield to fend off life's arrows of pain.

"Grandma, I can only have my *'nevers'* because I'm living here with you now. I love you, Grandma, for making it possible for me to make them disappear—one at a time."

She was full and overflowing when she heard my *'nevers'* and how much I loved her. I meant every word of it.

I was ashamed of Daddy. It would have been better if we could have blamed his actions on his drinking as Grandma wished. But, I decided I was not going to be mad at him for the mud episode. After seeing him work every day in the field next to me and after seeing how the tractor would lunge from one row to the next, I recognized the dangers of that horrible day. It was a scary thought that he could have run over me with that tractor. He didn't have to react so violently but...that was Daddy and that was how he reacted to almost everything.

Also, Grandma saying that Grandpa Omar was an abusive parent and taught my dad everything he knew gave me insight as to why he was prone to overreact to situations as he did.

I realized I was now rationalizing his actions just as Grandma does. I agree there was no excuse for his abuse to my mother. Neither of us would ever find justification for him for that.

I never had the *mud dream* again. Grandma helped me to piece the puzzle together, and that dream became another closed book. I was not going to blame my mother for feeding me like a little "fattening pig" either. She was just showing her love for me in a way that seemed right to her. To use Grandma's term of how Miss Katty showed her love for Sadie: it wasn't a wise love, but it was love...nonetheless.

Chapter Twenty-One

A Love Story Prevails

I T WAS SAD to say, but gossip about a murder was much more interesting than that of an accidental death. We didn't hear much about Nate McDougal anymore, though there were concerns of how Minnie would manage living alone out on Number Eight Ditch.

The adage *out of sight, out of mind* applied to most people, except to Grandma. She and Minnie created an even stronger bond after that meeting at Clete Oller's office.

It was a sight to see how Grandma was able to gather assistance from anyone who was willing to help make Minnie's place a little more livable. Daddy and a few other men in town repaired her roof. Mr. Simpson moved her pump to the porch. Asa bush-hogged the path to her house for easier access. Grandma visited her, every chance she got.

Despite of everyone's supportive efforts, Minnie continued to drift deeper into a state of depression. With each visit, Grandma said she would find her sitting in a motionless rocking chair and staring down the ditch bank where her only son had lost his life.

Nate had given his mother very little peace but had been her purpose for living all these years. If not to take care of Nate, Minnie said she could no longer feel as though she had a purpose or a reason to live.

Grandma shared with us about how on one particular day, she made her usual trek up the winding path to Minnie's house, to bring her some fried apple pies, a favorite comfort food of the South. Minnie was in her rocker, as usual.

"The bugs are bad this year, aren't they, Minnie?" Grandma reached for a little small talk, only to have it ignored.

"Tell Larson thank you for the kindling wood. I haven't done much cooking here lately, but I did use it to fire up the stove and make coffee this morning." Minnie mumbled incoherently.

Daddy might have had a lot of pent-up hatred for Nate, but he had genuine compassion for his mother. That tough as nails façade of my father's masked a soft heart on the inside, at least toward some people. Of course, what ever he did had to be his choice. If he took kindling to Minnie, no doubt it was his idea.

However, Grandma said she almost knew it had to be someone else who delivered the wood. Daddy had worked from sun-up to sun-down in Mr. Bertram's field all week long. However, if it made her feel better, she'd let Minnie think it was Daddy anyway.

Doing good deeds for others generally made a person feel better. Grandma recalled how that sparked an idea and a plan of how to lift her friend's spirits.

"Minnie, I need you to walk with me to Asa's field to take Larson and Meryl one of these pies for their dinner."

Minnie protested at first, but Grandma was very insistent.

"I don't feel good about taking that walk alone, Minnie. Will you do it as a favor to me?"

For the first time since Nate's death, Minnie felt needed. Her friend was asking her for a favor. Lord knows Grandma was there for her when she needed one. Minnie couldn't deny her, so the two of them set out to bring Daddy and me a pie.

On the way, Grandma said she tried to talk about anything other than Nate, but Minnie must have needed to vent. No matter how hard Grandma tried to avoid the subject, Minnie always brought it back to something about the death of her son.

"Alice, I wonder if seeing Nate fall to his death that night will always be the first thing I see in my mind in the morning and the last thing I see before I fall asleep at night?"

"Minnie, I can only imagine how losing your child must be the hardest thing you have ever had to go through. I truly believe and pray that God will help you find strength in this." These were not empty words. Grandma was sharing heart-filled feelings with her friend.

"I've questioned God many times for giving me a son such as Nate. Now I question Him even more, for taking him away, and wonder, 'Where is God in all of this?' I am just being honest. If I'm not taking care of Nate, I don't know what to do with myself. You always knew he didn't have what it took to take care of himself. Alice, I am not sure I can, or even want to go on or live."

"Minnie, you have no choice but to go on and live; and you will because you have to. There are just some things in this world that we won't ever understand until we can ask the Lord in person. I don't have all the answers for you, but I do know this much; God is in control. He is where He has always been. He never moved away from you. He had His reasons why He gave you Nate. I believe He knows who to give 'special children' to. Not everyone has strength enough to do what you did and how you did it, concerning Nate."

As Minnie was pondering what Grandma had just said about 'special children, Grandma continued with the message she felt she needed to present, "God's ways are not our ways. The Bible makes that very clear. God must have a purpose for you, or you wouldn't still be here. Same as me, I know now that my purpose is to do as right by Meryl Jean as possible. She is the little girl that God has finally chosen to give me. I want to measure up to His trust and handle that gift the best I can. I also want to do it for dear Edna. She loved Meryl so much. She was taken away at such an important time of that little girl's life." Grandma was talking to herself now as much to her friend.

"I know, Alice. She is such a dear child, and by what

I have seen so far, you are doing a good job with her. As for me, though, it is just me now. What am I to do? What…am…I to do?" She moaned as though all of Grandma's uplifting words had fallen on deaf ears.

Grandma finally got her attention. "Minnie, if you had died instead of Nate, what would you have wanted for him to do with what was left of his life?"

"Alice, Nate wasn't capable to do much with his life; he just lived it. I would have wanted someone to continue to let him do just that…live out the rest of his life. I hoped he could stay out of trouble and what life he had left would have been more peaceful since the first part was so troublesome."

"Then you must do the same, however you can do it. What you would have wanted for Nate should happen for you. You've earned it. He was a handful, but you took care of him his entire life. Now it is time to take care of Minnie. God will give you purpose if you'll be still and wait for Him to do it." Grandma was proclaiming the Scriptures to be truth and challenging Minnie to trust God and let Him work her situation out in His way and in His time.

The two of them fell silent until they reached the cotton field. Minnie knew that everything her wise friend had told her was the truth.

As they reached the field, they found Obe wrestling a heavy sack full of cotton onto the scales. Just as he turned around, he found himself face to face with Minnie. She recognized that he was the man Asa said had carried her to the porch, and she thanked him again.

He mumbled something about it being the least he could do, but this time, she was close enough to see his eyes.

He was making his way back to the field as she and Grandma started their search for Daddy and me. Suddenly, Minnie stopped, turned around, and softly asked, "Obadiah, is that you?"

Obe came to a halt, hesitated, and then turned around to face her again. It looked as though he might have wanted to run away but didn't. Instead, he shuffled his feet and confessed. "Yes, Minnie, it is me, Obadiah."

"It was you that carried me to the porch that night."

"Yes, I did."

"Obadiah, why didn't you say something…how long have you been here…where have you been all these years?"

"Guess we have some catchin' up to do."

"I can't believe it is you. I never knew what happened to you."

"Minnie, if it is ok with you; I'll come over after work and we can talk." By now, Obe saw they had a sizeable audience.

Mrs. Bertram, the girls, and I—along with several others—had made it to the end of our rows and were mesmerized by their conversation.

Mr. Bertram smiled and said, "Hey, Obe, why don't you just take the rest of the afternoon off. I'll let the girls finish out your row." Then, he told everyone to go back to work.

Normally the girls would have whined at the

thought of completing another person's job. That time, it didn't bother them at all to allow this long-lost couple privacy to reunite. I decided I would also offer to help them with Obe's row.

Minnie looked for Grandma's approval to leave with Obe, since she was there at her friend's request. Grandma was a helpless romantic at heart; of course, she told Minnie to go on, that she could find her way back home just fine. There was never a doubt that she could have done that anyway.

What happened next was to all of us onlookers, like having a front row seat in one of the sweetest movies ever made.

Obe gave Asa a nod of thanks, hurled his empty cotton sack over his shoulder, and Minnie and he walked off together. One would look at the other occasionally, as if seeking reassurance that they were not dreaming.

As we watched them make their way down the path toward the ditch, I decided all that audience needed was popcorn to make our *movie* complete!

Grandma wore a huge smile on her way to find Daddy and give him his fried apple pie. She gave him the one meant for me too since I was with the McCrady girls and she didn't have enough for them. She knew I wouldn't have wanted to selfishly eat a pie in front of them. She wished only to get Minnie off her front porch, out of her rocking chair, and nudge her toward an emotional healing. She never expected that day's turn of events, and felt blessed to be even a small part of it!

Yes, it was a good day that the Lord had made. She was rejoicing and glad in it.

While they sat beneath a huge oak tree and Daddy enjoyed his pies, she shared the sweetness of Obe and Minnie's reunion with him. In turn, he told her the complete story concerning the meeting in Clete's office. She was shocked to learn that 'Obe,' Obadiah, was Nate's real father and Zed McDougal's brother. That he was one of triplets was an equal shocker.

To think, all that time Obadiah and Minnie were right under each other's noses, and no one knew it but Obadiah himself.

After Asa told his wife the details of what was said in Clete's office, Emmy had a new opinion of Obadiah McDougal. She also had an idea of how to help make some changes in his life.

Carl Chaffin owned over half of Muddy Ox, which included the cotton gin. Mrs. Bertram had heard that he needed workers. She figured that she could summon a favor from Mr. Chaffin, since he was forever indebted to Asa. Obe needed a job, and Mr. Chaffin needed workers. It seemed like a simple solution to her scheme.

Obe first had to clean himself up. Surely there was a salvageable man underneath all the crud and hair on him. If so, Emerald Bertram was all about trying to find one. It wasn't fair to send him, or anyone else looking as he did, to ask Mr. Chaffin for a job.

She sized Obadiah and presented him with some new, clean clothes. She then offered their bath house so he could get a proper scrubbing. She first petitioned

Asa's assurance that he would clean up any mess that Obe left behind.

This was a meticulous woman who stripped every bed in her house and washed her linens every Saturday morning without fail. Even if it was a bath house, it too was kept spotless.

The transformation was miraculous! Anyone would have been willing to offer Obe a job if they went by appearances only. A bath, shave, hair cut, and new clothes did wonders for Obadiah.

Mrs. Bertram's plan worked out far beyond her greatest expectations. Obe not only got the job but was appointed group crew leader.

It wasn't long until Obadiah and Minnie were married as they probably should have been years before. Grandma and Daddy stood up with them at their wedding, and I sang. They both had found new purposes in life of loving and caring for each other.

Minnie now had someone she needed as much as they needed her. Grandma's words of comfort and wisdom often rang true in Minnie's ears. *"Be still and wait for God's purpose."*

The former Obe soon ceased to exist. Everyone called him Obadiah from then on; that was everyone except the members of his new crew who call him Mr. McDougal. Obadiah and I both had new names!

Grandma couldn't wait to get home and tell Katty every detail of her entire day. Perhaps she would ask Katty to wring a chicken's neck so she could fix some fried chicken for a celebration. Why, she might even ask

Miss Katty to wring two chicken's necks and invite their family for supper too. Katty could bring her pot of beans and hopefully whip up a cake. That would make for a really nice ending to the Lord's special day.

Miss Katty was just as surprised as Grandma to hear about Obe and Minnie's connection and reconciliation. She took her up on the offer of supper. Going into the pen, she caught two chickens, one in each hand and wrung both their necks at the same time. After passing them off to Grandma, she went home and started on her cake.

Once supper was over, Daddy and Mr. Simpson went out on the porch swing to smoke and talk. Simp smoked a pipe while Daddy puffed away on his cigarettes. Grandma and Miss Katty worked on the kitchen. Sadie sat in the floor and played jacks, while I got my sponge bath over with so I could enjoy cake with everyone afterward.

It was really good to see Mr. Simpson and Daddy talking together in the swing. Their renewed camaraderie in the aftermath of Nate McDougal's tragedy was encouraging and comforting.

After our supper guests went home, we all went straight to bed. While I lay in silence, the events of the day played in my head like a reel to reel tape. I had boarded the Bertram's wagon that morning the same as every other day. Even with my imagination, I could have never guessed what that day held in store for each of us in that cotton patch, much less what it held for Obe and Minnie. It gave me hope to think that not everything had to turn out sad or painful. It also made me see that it wasn't just the beautiful, handsome, wealthy, or the popular ones that found contentment and happiness. Neither Obe's or Minnie's shadow would be considered desirable to a lot of people, but their shadows were theirs and they were comfortable with them. They loved each other, in spite of themselves. From that time forward, I decided to try to view my shadow differently. I hoped to anyway.

The next day was Saturday, and that meant a half day in the field and the rest of the day in town. I only had a few more weeks to finish getting school things. I was anxious to see Polly again, show her my new clothes, and tell her about the summer's events.

Chapter Twenty-Two

The Tomcat Episode

J UST WHEN WE thought that Minnie and Obadiah had surprised us about as much as was possible, yet another surprise unfolded.

During their first reunion, Minnie revealed to Obadiah that he wasn't Nate's biological father after all. She had lost their baby shortly after he had left to find work. She conceived Nate shortly after she and Zed had gotten married. The evening that he was shot and killed, Zed was on his way to share that truth with Obadiah and settle their feud.

This was a huge relief to Obadiah. He had been haunted by thoughts of Minnie and the child he thought was his. He had often grieved about the severed relationship between him and his only living brother, Zedekiah.

It had been his choice to not to be a part of Minnie's and the child's lives after being freed from prison. Having been falsely accused of robbery made no difference about how Obadiah would be judged by everyone. He was tarnished with a prison record that would never go away. He chose not to have that mark hanging over the heads of those he loved. He thought that Minnie could have surely done better for herself than to have him in her life.

Obadiah had been guilt-ridden for years about neglecting his child. He felt even worse after having seen Nate's condition, and he thought it was a possible punishment for his and Minnie's past sins. He had also taken blame for leading Minnie astray on top of everything else. He would have stepped forward much sooner had he known that Minnie hadn't remarried after Zed's death. He was further anguished and felt he had made a mess of his, Minnie's and his child's lives. This was a tremendous heavy burden that he had carried for such a long time.

Minnie had no doubt been his life-long love. Maybe now he had been given a chance to make amends. Perhaps they'd both been given clean slates to better the rest of their lives.

The transition of Obadiah McDougal was something to see! He'd become a valuable crew leader at the cotton gin and had gained respect throughout the entire community. On Sundays, he and his new bride could often be seen leaving the little church on the edge of town. Obadiah thanked God every day for keeping Minnie safe and for their second chance. He no longer secretly left firewood on the porch but happily took it into their home and stacked it by the stove.

Mrs. Bertram accomplished what Grandma had asked her to do. She'd made a good field-hand out of me. I had been a little intimidated by her when we first met, but learned later that she could be a very kind and caring person. Her transformation of Obadiah McDougal had been proof of that.

My first season of cotton picking had gone very well. Picking two hundred and fifty pounds of cotton didn't happen for me every day to reach my goal, but I reached it as often as was possible.

My little closet was filled with a bounty of pretty school clothes. It also held enough girl shoes to last me throughout the winter and into spring, at least until chopping time came around again. By then, if they were needed, I could get more.

Working and buying my clothes and shoes, mostly by myself, gave me a tremendous sense of pride. It was mostly because Daddy had stayed around the entire season and added a few dollars to my purse almost every week. He also gave Grandma a little extra money from time to time. She put some back for us and used the rest toward the extra strain of having three mouths in the house. Daddy was doing better, but was still far from being an ideal father…whatever that was.

He didn't take as many *mysterious drives in the county* and to Grandma's and my surprise; he had repaired her chicken coop without having been asked.

Mr. Simpson and Daddy weren't as close as they might have been, but they seemed to find more common ground for small talk. So, some things changed, but some things remained the same. Daddy continued to have his crowd of drinking and hunting buddies, and we still had to contend with his occasional binges and quick temper.

One night in particular, Daddy had arrived home quite late from being supposedly at the auction in Doodlum Switch. He had been drinking heavily. He was tipsy, tired, and sleepy. All he wanted was to find his bed and fall into it.

The one old tom cat that Grandma kept around to rid us of field mice had slipped in behind Katty, unbeknownst to her or us, earlier that morning when she came by to return a cup of sugar. Grandma shooed the old cat out with a broom as soon as he was discovered, but not before he'd successfully deposited a little *gift* for her under the dresser in the corner of the bedroom.

Old Tom had relieved himself on the wood part of the floor that was just beyond the edge of the linoleum rug. After sniffing out the little pile pronto, Grandma scooped it up and quickly got it outside. The offensive mess being on the wood part of the floor made for a more difficult clean up.

Grandma scrubbed the spot several times, first with detergent, then with a baking soda paste, and then poured a little rubbing alcohol on it, hoping it might take care of any lingering odor.

She repeated the process about two hours later, just because. Another one of her favorite sayings was, "Any job worth doing, do it with all your might. If it is worth doing at all, it is worth doing right!" Grandma practiced what she preached.

Pulling the dresser away from the wall, she hoped the water-soaked wood would dry more quickly. The oblong table that sat between her and Daddy's beds, in their shared bedroom, was also moved clear of the drenched spot. Once the floor had dried, everything could go back into its rightful place.

Daddy made it home about 2:30 am, and proceeded to stumble into bed. To avoid waking Grandma and having to endure her questions and scolding, he never turned on the overhead light. Of course, Grandma, being a very light sleeper and one who never slept soundly until she was satisfied of his safe arrival, always knew when he got home and only pretended to be sleeping. She didn't wish to upset him at that hour of the morning any more than he wanted her lectures.

Unfortunately, that time everything went awry. After kicking out of his shoes and removing his socks, he slipped off his pants to lay them on the oblong table as usual, only to hear them hit the floor. He figured he must surely have been drunker than he thought to have missed the table completely. Bending over to retrieve his pants, he bumped his head on the edge of the dresser that was still pulled away from the corner of the wall.

Stumping his toe on the metal roller of the dresser foot, he stumbled backwards onto the soppy wet floor and became even more angry and confused. That…was when the cussing began!

It was way more than he could deal with in his condition and in the dark; so he finally pulled the string to turn on the light. It came on, but the string broke. By that time, as a result of the uproar from Daddy's raring and swearing, every house within earshot was lit up, and all of the dogs in the neighborhood were howling.

Grandma bounced out of bed and tried to explain the situation to her drunken son, who was by then, clad only in his underwear and nursing a huge bump on his head.

I, who could usually sleep through a train wreck, was awakened and ran to see what was wrong with Daddy and Grandma.

Miss Katty, in her nightgown and Simp with a shotgun in his trembling hands, were standing on their back porch, trying to gather clues as to the cause of our ruckus. Simp was truly wishing it was just one of Daddy's drunken capers and not a situation that needed some neighborly intervention. He owned the gun, and had it in his hands but had no desire to have to use it. Grandma saw them and gave them a wave of "all clear." They both breathed a quiet sigh of relief and returned inside their house.

Daddy had a few choice words for the cat and threatened to kill it if he ever saw it again. Grandma begged him not to blame the poor dumb cat because it didn't know any better. Then, she took blame for everything and said she was sorry for not putting the room back in place.

Finally, everyone settled down. The neighbors' houses were dark again and the dogs got quiet once more. Grandma got a cool rag for Daddy's head, and they both finally got settled down.

Straining mightily to muffle my giggles, I too returned to bed. The whole thing happened just because Daddy didn't want to wake us by turning on the light. Instead, he woke up half of Silver Leaf and possibly a portion of Muddy Ox!

He wasn't angry as we feared he would be the next morning. Instead, he had a new comical story to tell for many years. He wasn't in the habit of laughing at himself, but the cat and table incident almost always brought a smile.

Daddy left shortly after breakfast to take a part for Mr. Bertram's plow to the blacksmith shop in Doodlum Switch. The tomcat that caused the commotion was sleeping lazily on the back porch. As Daddy passed by, he couldn't resist stomping loudly a few inches away from the old cat's tail. Of course it howled and ran for cover. Daddy stuck his head back in the door and said, "That cat cost me a good night's sleep and a bump on my head. It isn't fair that he gets to sleep if I can't."

Grandma and I could hardly wait until he got out of sight before bursting into full belly-laughs. We were both relieved and amused at Daddy's oddly good natured attitude with the whole affair.

He came in drunk many times after that and still didn't turn on the light for the obvious reasons; but before taking off his pants, he always checked to see if the table was where it belonged, just to be safe. The knot on his head lasted for at least a week or more. He then realized he couldn't take anything for granted, not even the predictability of his own usually very predictable mother.

Chapter Twenty-Three

Meeting Another Challenge

M Y NEXT BIGGEST challenge was going to be to convince my extremely conservative Grandma that I needed to wear a little of what she disgustedly called powder and paint. *The* McCrady sisters and the other girls wore makeup to school. The last thing I wanted was to be different. School would be starting in a few days; so I needed to come up with some convincing words—and soon.

Daddy left for the auction in Doodlum Switch again soon after supper. Grandma and I found our usual place in the swing once the kitchen was cleaned.

The evening brought a chill to the air, giving a prediction of winter days not far behind. We wouldn't be sitting outside long that night.

The bulk of the cotton crop had been harvested. Any crop left in the fields was referred to as *rough cotton*. The baking sun of summer was tamed and the cool temperatures resulted in partially opened cotton bolls. Husks that once hugged the fluffy locks were dry and hardened with completely unforgiving sharp points.

Gloves were no longer anyone's choice or a hindrance; they were a necessity. The procedure for harvesting any straggling cotton remaining in the fields was referred to as *pulling*. All rules were set aside for *pulling*. Husk, leaves, partially open bolls and even tiny stalks were allowed since it was nearly impossible to get the cotton otherwise. Farmers received less money per bale for pulled cotton, but it was better than letting it go to waste in the fields. Besides, they needed every penny they could get.

PULLING WAS LEFT up to the men and a few determined women who insisted on working shoulder to shoulder beside their men until the last stalk of cotton was pulled and the last possible dollar could be made.

All students were required to return to school for the new term. We made our last Saturday trip to town for the season. This was it, ready or not, and I was ready.

I just had that one little challenge still lurking ahead of me.

"Are you looking forward to school starting next week? You think you have about everything you need?" Grandma was pretty sure she knew the answer but asked anyway.

"Yes, I'm ready. I can't wait to see Polly and to wear all of my new clothes and tennis shoes to school." I was hoping against hope that Polly's dad had not moved them away in search of another harvest somewhere.

"Are you worried about being in the ninth grade and in high school now? Hard to believe this summer has gone by so fast. I'm proud of how you took to working in the cotton field, Meryl. Mrs. Bertram says you needed a bit of breaking in but you turned out to be a good little field hand."

Maybe this was the opening I needed to address the make-up issue; the worse thing she could say is no. So I began.

"Grandma, now that I am fourteen and going into high school do you think I might be able to wear a little lipstick like the other girls? I would wear it real light. The McCrady girls wear some and so do most of the other girls at school. I know you don't think much of girls wearing make up. But, as long as I don't look like a clown, do you think I could wear some, maybe just a little bit anyway?" I tried to get it all out before she could break in and object.

"Now, Meryl Jean," she started.

"Oh, Grandma, please, all the other girls wear it, and I don't want to be different. I already have enough of a problem being overweight and different. If you say I can, Daddy will maybe be ok with it too."

At first, I thought she was going to say no, but then surprisingly she agreed to let me wear *just a little bit*, as long as I stuck to my promise and didn't make myself look like a clown or a floozy.

I had heard about floozies but of course had never

seen one. From the frown on Grandma's face when she said the word "floozy," I decided I surely didn't want to look like one. I had seen clowns, and it seemed to me that they brought a lot of attention to themselves. Attention, especially the wrong kind, was the last thing I wanted to bring to my—maybe *now, I hoped*—a little less of a shadow.

We had another long talk to get a clear understanding of where we both stood concerning me and makeup. Grandma admitted that she knew she needed to be more broad-minded about a few things. She'd never worn p*aint* a day in her life, but times had changed since she was a girl.

She said that her mother had strictly frowned upon girls wearing dresses above their ankles. Grandma and her sisters were required to wear long sleeves and their bodices be buttoned up to the collar of their dresses. Even as children, they were forbidden to wear the color red, because her mother believed that red was the color the fancy ladies downtown wore to attract men. To that day almost every dress Grandma owned was either brown, black, dark blue or purple. There were no pinks, light blues, yellows or—heaven forbid—reds in her modest clothes closet.

Yes, times had changed. Although she remained discreet about the dresses she chose, Grandma confessed she had learned it wasn't the color of garments worn on the *outside* but what was on their *inside* that defined people. She decided she could shape me into a modest lady without imposing such harsh restrictions.

I squealed upon hearing her say yes! Then, I confessed I had already bought a little make-up during our last trip to town. Grandma said she guessed as much, and told me to go put some on, so she could see what she had just agreed to.

After carefully applying a minimal amount of makeup for what I knew was going to be a very judgmental pair of eyes, I made my debut.

"See, Grandma, it doesn't make me look bad. I promise I will only put it on lightly. This pale pink is the kind that Tara and Melly wear. What do you think?"

Grandma said she was surprised at the difference it made on my face. The slightly pink tinge enhanced and softly sculpted what used to be my dimpled baby-face but was now becoming the face of a fashionable young lady.

Grandma could see how much it meant to me to look more like the other girls, especially the McCrady girls. She had never seen anything disrespectful out of them; if there had been, Emerald Bertram would have straightened them out immediately.

She agreed that if I didn't wear any more makeup than what she was looking at, it would be ok. She also warned that she would be taking notice of my face every morning before I left for school. I hugged her and thanked her for seeing how important that was for me. I happily went to wash my face and get ready for bed. I was thinking that possibly asking to listen to Elvis, Rock N Roll music and getting a pair of pink pedal pushers should wait 'til later.

I had no doubt that in addition to her usual prayer that night, Grandma asked God to give her special wisdom and patience when making decisions concerning me. She had told me many times that she and her Maker had a good understanding of her role in my life and the responsibilities that came with it.

From the sound of her iron-frame bed squeaking once she went to bed, it was evident that she was tossing and trying to put her body to rest but her mind was still very much awake. I knew she was wrestling with her decision and was hoping she had done the right thing with me and the makeup choice.

She had promised to monitor my appearance often and I knew she would follow through. Before she agreed to let me experiment with make-up she quoted another of her little proverbs about giving me an inch and she didn't intend on me taking a mile from it. She closed her mini-sermon with the biblical scripture warning that it was the *little foxes that spoiled the vine*.

I had over-heard her tell Katty that girl-raising might not be so easy after all. She said she would have to pick her battles as she had always had to do with her sons. It was just going to be different kinds of battles.

Grandma often reminded me that there wasn't a doubt in her mind that God had a hand in my being placed in her care. She shared a conversation she'd had with my Uncle Paul, her youngest son, who'd grown up to become a minister. His counsel to her after Grandpa Omar's death was similar to the encouragement she'd had tried to give Minnie during their walk to the field that day they came to bring Daddy and me our pies.

Grandma said her son Paul told her that until after Grandpa Omar had died, she had never been privileged to be her own person and think for herself. She had gone from being a little girl of fourteen, living in her mother's household, to fifty-six years of being held under the thumb of a dominating husband, eleven years older than she.

She and Paul discussed that Grandpa Omar's background was very different from hers. Grandma had been raised in a peaceful home, governed by a resourceful, kind and loving widowed mother. Her mother feared and trusted God and was determined to raise Grandma and her sisters to do the same.

Omar's mother was also a war-widow but had a hard heart. To unscrupulously fight and scratch for everything she could get, with no regard to others' feelings or pain, was not beneath her. She was of the opinion that God never gave anyone anything. If they got it—they took it themselves. Brute force was her tool of choice, and she raised all her children to think the same way. Grandma confessed that was probably why Grandpa was such a hard man and was probably also why he was so physically and mentally abusive to her and their sons.

Until she met Omar, Grandma's circle of life was very small. She had never been exposed to Omar's kind of people. Grandma said she realized that Grandpa had never even heard of the Golden Rule of treating others as you would want to be treated, much less, living by it. She conceded that he treated her in most ways on equals with their sons. He controlled the money, the household and Grandma.

Her entire life was wrapped around her husband, his wishes, his comfort and his rule. She'd never known what it was to make decisions alone. Grandma had seen their finances only a quarter at a time. It wasn't that she didn't like having her newly found freedom—but she confessed that at the time, she was merely confused as to what to do with it.

Grandma said Paul's advice prompted her to face her fears and unhappiness, soon after Grandpa's death. She hadn't known why God took him and left her behind. She thought she was a burden to her family because of her fear of spending nights alone and the challenge of handling responsibilities that she'd never had before. Feelings of inadequacy loomed, along with a lack of self-worth, causing her to not understand why she was still alive.

Grandma said that Paul's words still rang true as when he reminded her of how very much alive she was and that she was smarter than she thought. He had encouraged her to count her blessing of good physical and mental health and to use her freedom to do as she chose for the first time in her life.

He suggested that her purpose or mission wasn't complete if even one of her sons was estranged from God. Grandma said after her talk with Paul, she woke up the next day and every day after that feeling better about why she was still on this earth.

It was Uncle Paul who suggested that Grandma might spend nights with the Simpsons since they lived so close by. Simp and Katty were happy for her to stay nights at their house. They often said how they felt more like Grandma's own children than mere neighbors.

Once I came to live with Grandma, we stayed at home at night. She told Katty that she had decided that I had enough of both of my parents in me that I was not much afraid of anything, except maybe stinging worms. She felt a little ashamed that having a brave child, barely in her teens, in her house made her feel safe enough to stay there after all.

After Grandma told me the details of her and Uncle Paul's talk, I realized that he was able to paint what remained of her life on a canvas that let her see it more clearly. Having me added to her life's mission gave her an even more important reason to still be alive.

I listened as soft prayers came from Grandma's bedroom. After praying again for each of her sons and their families, she added for God to help her pick up where my mother had left off with me. After thanking God for another good day, she drifted into a peaceful night's rest.

I said a little thankful prayer myself, for God helping Grandma to decide to let me wear make-up, my closet full of new clothes, and—my girl shoes.

Chapter Twenty-Four

Reflections

T HOSE FOURTEEN MONTHS of my life from August
1959 to October 1960 seemed like an eternity then
but eventually I have come to see them as only a
moment in time.

When school started, my life resumed its usual pattern. Grandma and I had always known traveling fever
would get to Daddy eventually. He was never a fan of
field work to begin with, and pulling cotton was
especially unappealing to him. With the crop over with,
there wasn't much left for him to do around Muddy Ox
during the winter months. Daddy had said he might go
to Florida, where work was abundant year round. It
seemed he had changed a bit—but then again, not. I
guessed Daddy would always just be…Daddy.

Even today, I still remember the tiny bit of selfish
sadness I felt that morning as I walked by where
Daddy's car had usually been parked. The threat of
colder days ahead was hovering around the corner, but
that day was what Mr. Simpson would have called
tolerable. As I waved good-bye to Grandma and started

down the gravel lane toward school, I thought how I would miss Daddy dropping me off on school mornings occasionally—most definitely when winter set in.

During my solo walks to school I usually had done a lot of thinking. If there was going to be a test that day, I'd sometimes quiz myself until I could get with Polly so we could quiz each other. Fortunately, her dad had chosen to stay put for a while; so they hadn't moved. Polly and I had kept our fingers crossed that his job would be a permanent one—at least for three more years.

I was proud of my academic achievements since moving to Muddy Ox School. Having a calmer, more structured home life had helped me to become a better student. It's never easy for a child to settle down and learn at school after just leaving a storm at home.

I think even at thirteen I knew there had always been something inside me that wanted to do well in whatever I did. I might have gotten it from my mother, but I have decided it was being nurtured by Grandma.

I was equally fearful and excited about starting my freshman year in high school and what the months ahead, along with the next three years, would hold for me. Would I become one of those giggly girls in the ice cream parlor? Would a special someone peek through the window for a glimpse of me? Would I someday be part of the 'in-crowd' as Tara and possibly be invited to join Beta Club? Would another 'Hezzie' rise up and see me as a target? If so, what would be my next act of defense, and would my guardian angel again come to my rescue?

On a larger scale, as Grandma had wondered about the hardships I'd be facing in the cotton fields, I wondered what challenges awaited me once I left those cotton fields and tiny Muddy Ox in search of a bigger world.

I hoped one day to have the opportunity to sing for an audience larger than a church congregation, but also for one who would enjoy and hold on to every note, just as they did.

Beyond just adopting a new name, I had experienced many other changes. Daddy might have brought an intimidated little Meryl to Muddy Ox but each time he returned home from one of his adventures, he was met with a more self-assured and happier Jean.

I had learned many life-lessons in such a short span of time. Although I never knew him personally, my encounter with the curious eyes of Nate McDougal taught me that we may hate the deeds, but we should never judge someone without first knowing the driving forces behind that person. I learned a similar lesson from 'Obe', Obadiah McDougal. As Daddy had said, "Once all the life that was hanging on him got removed, there was actually an 'alright' guy underneath it all." I guess that can be true in all of us. After all, Grandma always said that is what salvation is about.

It is undoubtedly from Grandma that I had learned the most. Living with her, and seeing the woman she really is, had taught me first of all, that one's worth or intelligence is not defined by material things or formal education. Grandma always taught me that character is what remains when everything that doesn't belong in the first place is chiseled away. She truly believed that the light of God could live within a soul and ultimately shine through to make that soul a more vivid reflection of Him.

I have found forgiveness toward my mother and father. Once all of the pieces of my puzzling past were put in place, I could see the picture in its entirety to understand what caused them to do as they did. Having come to grips with that, I must say I always wanted more than either of them settled for in their own lives— and still do.

I am a *work in progress* as I struggled then, and continue to struggle, to forgive my Grandpa Omar. I might be able to give him credit for saving my life, the day he made the hole in my bottle nipple larger, but it is hard to forgive him for how he treated Grandma. It is also difficult to forgive the calloused rearing that left my Daddy with so many sharp edges to his personality. Again, I will have to try to be more tolerant toward Grandpa Omar, knowing that his foundation was formed by his unfortunate upbringing and the voids in his life as well.

As I look back, I can just say that for the most part, any goodness about him was largely because he co-existed with Grandma for fifty-six years. After all, look what an impact I've always known she had on me, especially during the time I had been fortunate enough to live with her.

As for me personally, although my shadow still remains larger than I would wish it to be, I have found that it is not the size of the shadow a person makes, it is the size of the impression that shadow leaves, once it has passed over something or someone.

However unpleasant they were at the time, I am now thankful for my 'nevers.' They helped to replace the constraints of intimidation with open doors of confidence. More 'nevers' are being added to my life as it evolves. But as for the ones I brought with me to Grandma's house, in August of 1959, I can say that most of those 'nevers' were resolved, and if by chance any of them do remain—I'm still working on them.

The whirlwind that day in the cotton patch when Tara told me to throw back my bonnet will always be a defining experience. I have come to realize there are many different kinds of whirlwinds. Some are good and refreshing, and some just catch us up within their forces until time to set us down again.

If this year and two months was only a hint of what lay ahead for me, then I must forever "WATCH FOR THE NEXT WHIRLWIND" to see where it would pick me up and pray I'll be ready for when or wherever it sets me down again. There's no way to know which kind of future 'whirlwind' I'll be facing—but I know there will be one waiting for me down the next path I choose to take.

The End

Nahum 1:3 "the Lord has His way in the whirlwind and in the storm."

Dedication

I dedicate this above all to God who has always been in the midst of the "whirlwinds" of my life. I dedicate this to my Grandmother, who was the inspiration for the grandmother in this story. Finally—and most important—I dedicate this to "Lou, My Love," my husband who believed in me as I promised him when we first met, that I always had this book in me. I wish he could have lived to see that promise kept.

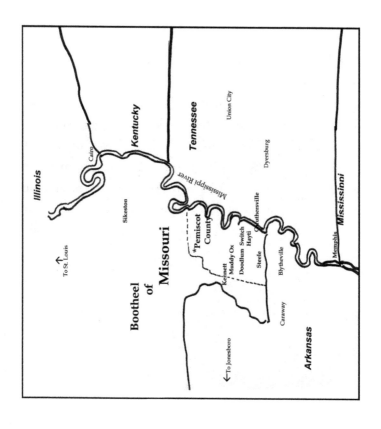

Acknowledgments

Thank you to my many friends and family members for reading and editing my manuscript early on. I want to give special thanks to Robin Kinser, Jeff Treece, Karen Treece, Pauline Evans, Marta Brumley, Brenda Vincent, Wesley Self, Jacquelyn Self, Yuvawn Love, Linda Garcia, Bonnie Causey and Rev. Joe Causey, for your support and encouragement in this endeavor.

Thank you Rick Ashby for the countless hours we spent over coffee hashing out the facts and possibilities for my characters and story line and for introducing me to Charmaine. Good luck with your future book also. Thank you to the managers and employees at Hardees on Russellville Road in Bowling Green, Kentucky, for your interest and kinds words of encouragement as well, while watching this book progress.

I appreciate the objective critiquing from Jesse Knifley and those who are a part of our writing workshop at the Warren County Public Library, Bowling Green, Kentucky. Good luck to all of you in your writing projects.

I want to extend a very special thank you to Dr. Charmaine Allmon Mosby, my chief editor and advisor. Charmaine went home to be with the Lord October 25,

2014. I am so sorry she never got to see the finished project.

1 Thessalonians 5:18, tells us to give thanks in all circumstances, for this is God's will for us in Christ Jesus. I want to thank God for allowing the many circumstances that I refer to as whirlwinds in my own life that I could reflect upon them while writing Meryl's story. After reading *Watch for the Whirlwinds*, if just one reader can find peace with their circumstances—past and or present—and forgiveness for those who brought them about, then I feel as though I have done what I was supposed to do by writing this book.

About the Author

NOEL BARTON moved around quite a bit as a child but spent her teen years in the Bootheel of Missouri after her mother's death to cancer. She now resides in Bowling Green, Kentucky. She is a mother, grandmother, widowed (twice), best friend to her little dog Zacchaeus and a retired travel counselor. Being a devout Christian, she credits God for her writing ability and is very active in her church and its activities. **Watch for the Whirlwinds** is her first novel. Although, not an autobiography, many aspects of the book are pulled from personal experiences. It is her wish that those reading **Watch for the Whirlwinds** will find peace to cross off some the 'never's in their lives.